CW01095629

MARIKKA

Sam Hawksmoor

Hammer & Tong
UK

Hammer & Tong

Hammer & Tong
UK
www.samhawksmoor.com

Publisher's Note: This is a work of fiction. Names, characters, places,
and incidents are a product of the author's imagination. Locales
and public names are sometimes used for atmospheric purposes.
Any resemblance to actual people, living or dead, or to businesses,
companies, events, institutions, or locales is completely coincidental.

Marikka / Sam Hawksmoor - 1st ed.

ACKNOWLEDGEMENTS

For Karen Savage who's encouragement was invaluable
And the City of Vigo where I found the right coffee bar to begin
Marikka's story
And Evie West, born this year and has so much to look forward to …
And finally Dominic Robson for his patience in designing this book

REVIEWS FOR SAM HAWKSMOOR

THE REPOSSESSION TRILOGY
Winner of The Wirral 'Paperback of the Year' – 2013 'Without a doubt, one of the best YA Sci Fi series out there' Evie Seo - Bookish

THE REPERCUSSIONS OF TOMAS D
'Terrific fast paced read. Highly recommend for teens / YA / and adults too!' Carine on Goodreads.com

ANOTHER PLACE TO DIE: THE ENDTIME CHRONICLES
'Beautiful, plausible, and sickeningly addictive, Another Place to Die will terrify you, thrill you, and make you petrified of anyone who comes near you...' Roxy Williams - Amazon.co.uk

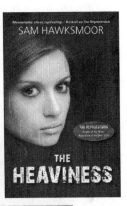

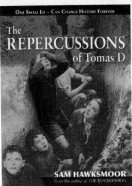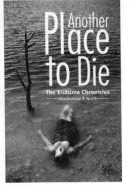

ONE

A DOGS DINNER

Marikka woke suddenly, the echo of a broken dream still swimming in her head. It was a warm night, the air unusually thick and cloying. She found she'd kicked the blankets off the bed. She looked down for Deacon, puzzled he wasn't sprawled on the floor as usual. With a sudden sense of guilt she remembered why.

She'd gone to bed early with a headache. Deacon had been tied up beside the stables as punishment for biting her little stepbrother's football. He'd only wanted to play, but the dog had very sharp teeth. Her stepfather had beaten him and tied him up, telling them he wasn't to have food or water for two whole days. That was her stepfather all over. Always making rules, always beating something or someone. She never understood why her mother had married him. If he wasn't shouting at Marikka, he was yelling at anyone who came to the house. He seemed to be a perpetually angry man.

This airless night was part of a late summer heatwave. The local farmers had all been frantic to get the harvest in before the rains came back. That was the other thing. Her stepfather lived in a big old crumbling farmhouse in the country. Imagined himself gentry in his tweeds, green wellies and slightly battered Range Rover. He often went out with his pals shooting pheasants or anything that moved.

His family had lived here at the Grange for generations he claimed. Mrs Bridges at the newsagents in Brigstock had told Marikka that ten years back he'd been an ordinary local tractor driver who'd got lucky in an auction. The Grange owner had died suddenly and the families were desperate to get rid of the old draughty farmhouse. Business was bad though, the taxman was breathing down his neck for unpaid taxes and she knew he had mounting debts.

Her mother wasn't good at facing reality, but clearly he wasn't the rich man he'd led her to believe he was and she took it out on Marikka. 'Everything started to go wrong when you came back,' was the usual accusation she flung at her. Her mother always took her stepfather's side in any arguments. Little love was won or lost in this house.

The house was eerily quiet. Marikka pulled on her jeans and a light sweater, slipping on old and comfortable purple Converse sneakers. She checked her phone – 1.30am. She felt safe enough. Everyone would be asleep. Deacon needed to be fed and he'd be really thirsty. You can't tie up a Ridgeback and just ignore its piteous whining. The dog was absolutely dedicated to Marikka and she felt personally responsible for his fate since she'd been kicking the stupid ball to him in the first place.

The stairs creaked. She listened. No one stirred.

She reached *their* bedroom. The door open, she glanced in. Her mother was asleep, mouth open, flat on her back – but her stepfather wasn't there!

Her heart began to beat wildly. Where was he? He normally lay there snoring so loudly that she always thought of him like a pig in a blanket beside her mother. And now he wasn't there! Where was he? In the loo? She listened, but heard nothing. Downstairs in the kitchen? She had to help Deacon, she felt so guilty.

Where was her stepfather? Of course he may have gone drinking with his friends at The Green Dragon. He often came home late, wrecked, then woke with a mean temper in the morning. That was it. He must have gone drinking... or ...

In the kitchen she scooped up dog biscuits into a bowl, filled an empty two-litre milk carton with fresh water and then snuck out, careful to leave the back door ajar.

She looked up, happy to see stars. That was the most amazing thing about living in the country. She'd never seen many stars in London skies and remained in awe of them, wishing she knew their names.

Deacon heard her approaching of course. He was already wagging his tail, his whole body shaking from side to side with happiness, although it had to hurt with the beating he'd had earlier.

'Hey boy, brought you dinner and water. Go easy now. OK?'

Deacon ignored her and stuck his head into the bowl and speedily chomped away. He wasn't going to risk the food being taken away again. When he drank he practically drowned himself he swallowed so much. It must have been a very hot day behind the stables.

Marikka squatted down on the dirt next to him, reluctant to go back to the house. The air was cooler out here and she'd missed her dog. He always slept in her room. The only protection she had against the world.

'I'm sorry he's so mean,' she told him, stroking his soft ears.

Deacon nuzzled her as she untied him. The dog would need a walk; he'd been tethered on a tight leash to the wall.

'Come on.'

They were in the woods when they heard a vehicle approaching. Nothing too strange about that, except it being nearly two in the morning. Normally Deacon would have barked, woken the whole house up. But she kept him quiet.

Headlights briefly illuminated the trees. Marikka sensed they were coming towards the house. If they were coming to the house, they'd be bringing her stepfather back, and if he discovered she was out of bed and feeding Deacon there would be hell to pay.

'We stay here.' She told him, worried now. The dog pressed against her. He was anxious. Late visitors always meant trouble for him.

Hopefully they'd drop her stepfather off and go. With luck he'd never know she wasn't in the house. It wasn't unusual for strange men to come visiting the house at night. She had no idea what her stepfather was up to, but she sensed it wasn't legal. She waited with Deacon. Would wait all night if necessary.

About ten minutes later a Landrover came driving out of the grounds at speed, careering along the bumpy track through the woods, heading for the back road. Only a local or someone who knew the farmhouse well could possibly know that the track was there.

Deacon and Marikka shrank back into the trees as the Landrover bounced past them on the uneven track.

Why were they leaving in such a hurry? She shrank back further, but someone was looking out of the side window, and just for one brief second, their eyes met. Marikka had a shock. She dismissed it the moment it happened. Perhaps he hadn't seen her, but why was her stepfather still in the back of the Landrover with them? Couldn't be. She had to have imagined it. Yet, for that snatched moment, their eyes had definitely met. Could he have known it was her? Impossible in the darkness surely, but she'd know his terrible brooding eyes anywhere.

Deacon sensed trouble first, wanting to break free of her grip. She could suddenly smell smoke, heady with a stink of petrol. Heard the crackling fire.

They ran in panic for the house, all fear of being discovered gone. Deacon's ears were pricked back as he ran ahead barking.

They swung around the stables and standing before them the whole house was burning. The stench of petrol was overpowering. Whoever they were, they had deliberately set this fire and meant it to take quickly.

'Ma?' She screamed. Her window was open. She had to be able to hear her.

Marikka ran for the front door, but that was already burning too fiercely for her to get close. She ran to the rear of the house, but found the backdoor she had carefully left ajar was now locked. The old house was burning fast. They had made sure of it.

'Mum? Steven!' She screamed again. The roar of the flames was building in strength. She shouted for them again, but got no reply.

Why couldn't they hear her?

She threw a brick through the kitchen window. It bounced off. Double-glazing is hard to break with just one brick. She threw it again with more force. This time it shattered.

There was an explosion somewhere in the house. Flames shot through the living room consuming everything in its path. No way her mother could have slept through that. She climbed up to the window and kicked the glass in. Deacon howled outside, doing his best to wake everyone.

She was in the kitchen running the taps but no water came out. *They'd shut the water off.*

She ran for the door even though she could see flames licking under it. She tried the metal handle but it was too hot to touch already.

'Ma! Steven! Wake up. Get out.'

She remembered the old back stairs that would have been used by kitchen staff in years gone by.

She opened the door and a ton of old books fell out. She found the light switch, nothing happened. *They'd cut the power as well.* These people had known exactly what to do and where everything was.

There was a phone on the wall, but even as she lifted it she knew it would be dead. She remembered her precious mobile was upstairs by her bed. Useless now.

Smoke engulfed the kitchen. But she had to try to get up those stairs. She had to wake her mother. It was impossible that she could still be sleeping.

She clamboured over the books, made her way through the smoke and darkness to the door up ahead. But when she got there and tried to open it, dense acrid smoke filled the stairwell and she began to choke. She had to get out onto the landing and pulled her sweater over her head to stop her hair from burning. Blue flames rapidly spread like a poured liquid across the landing carpets as everything ignited around her.

'Mum! Steven!' She screamed again, rushing into her mother's bedroom. To her astonishment the room was empty, the bedclothes heaped on the floor. She heard a car horn blast outside and rushed to the window.

Her mother was sitting in her Mini-Countryman wearing her dressing gown, little Steven beside her. Their eyes connected and her mother lowered her window as Marikka pushed up the sash window. Bad idea. Flames were sucked into the room and Marikka knew there was no way back.

Her mother's face was twisted in anger. 'You wicked, wicked girl. You did this. After all we did for you and this is how you repay us? May you burn in hell, Marikka. May you burn in hell!'

Marikka was astonished. She was about to protest her innocence, but flames seemed to leap across the room towards her and with a shriek she had to run into the bathroom. Her mother had already driven off.

She was shaking now. How could anyone think she had done this? She slammed the bathroom door behind her. There was an interconnecting door to the guest room, but no escape beyond that. She ran into the guest room and shut that door too, aware that flames were already in the corridor behind it.

She still couldn't believe her mother had driven off and blamed her for this. Sure there was that stupid incident when she was nine and she'd accidentally burned the garden shed down the night before Guy Fawkes, but surely...

She struggled with the sash window. It had to be opened. It had to be. It finally slid up and stuck fast. She looked out. Deacon was looking for her, whimpering with anxiety.

'Deacon!'

He was there below her and she worried that if she jumped she'd break both their necks for sure.

She discovered that there was a drainpipe close enough to grab. It was that or nothing. She turned around and squeezed out of the window backwards, leaning over to get a handle on the pipe. She hoped it would hold her weight.

Deacon barked encouragement as she slid her legs out and began to shimmy down the rusted metal pipe. There was a sudden cracking noise below her and flames shot out of the window below. Deacon yelped and backed off. Marikka had no choice but to keep climbing down, struggling with grip and where to put her feet.

As she passed the lower window she could see into the house and was astonished by the immense heat as the inferno grew in strength.

The pipe suddenly broke away from the wall and she fell the last six feet to the ground, hurting her back. She swore loudly, wincing with pain, as she gasped for breath.

Deacon was beside her in a flash, tugging at her jacket, trying to get her away.

She rolled over, pains in her chest and back, but knew she had to move away from the building fast. The house was already shedding masonry and shards of hot shattered glass, which fell all around them.

She dragged herself away, almost doubled up with the struggle to breathe.

She still couldn't believe her mother had just automatically assumed it was her who'd done this and driven off. Left her to perish in the fire. What kind of mother would do that? Hers, of course. Always ready to blame her for anything and everything that went wrong in life.

'Run, Deacon.' He needed no telling, but looked back to make sure she was following.

Marikka was conscious her hands and fingers were scraped and sore, but she didn't care. She was sorry she'd gone back for her mother. Sorry she and Deacon hadn't run away like they'd planned to a hundred times or more in the last few months. Now she didn't know whether to stay or go. Her mother would soon be telling the police that she'd started the fire, that Marikka was a firebug. Just because of what she did aged nine. All she'd wanted was to get the sparklers to work, but somehow all the fireworks had caught and next thing she knew was that the whole shed was on fire.

From that moment on everything had changed in her life. Her father was dead, killed in a road accident. She wasn't even allowed to keep her old surname, her mother hated her father so much. Her mother was unable to cope with her, she told the social workers, and she was sent away. Besides, she'd met this man, Mr Stander, and Marikka was suddenly an inconvenience. She was only allowed home three years later, long after her mother had married Stander and moved to his big house. 'He will discipline you,' her mother had told her. 'Keep you in check'.

'We're bloody well going this time, Deacon,' she declared. 'I'm never going to another foster home ever again.'

The whole house was burning behind her, flames belching from every window. Every few seconds something exploded or shattered and the roar of the flames was almost deafening. Who knew a house could make so much noise when it died?

She saw headlights coming towards her. Perhaps it was the farmer from across the way? She waved. Too late she saw that it was the same Landrover that had been there before.

A shot rang out. Hit the barn wall behind her with a loud smack. Shot gun.

Marikka couldn't believe she was being shot at. She began to run in a zig-zag fashion. Deacon running besides her, not understanding, his ears flat, panic in his paws.

'Run, Deacon. Run!'

The second shot grazed her shoulder and she stumbled a little, but she darted behind the garden wall and didn't stop, crouching as she ran as fast as she could to the far end of the garden and then into the ditch.

'Back to the woods, boy. Back to the woods.' Deacon needed no encouragement, but he stuck close beside her.

She glanced back. A man with a powerful flashlight was moving quickly towards the ditch.

Who were these people chasing her?

Another shot rang out. She heard Deacon yelp and turn to bite his back.

They had shot Deacon!

She stopped a moment, felt his back. It was sticky with blood, but it was just a graze, he'd live. She made him get up and together they crawled out of the ditch.

They were near the stables again. Luckily her horse had been sold off six months before. These buildings would be next to burn.

'Can you see her?' Someone shouted.

'The bitch is out here somewhere, and she's got the dog.'

'Come on, we have to go.'

'Can't leave her as a witness.'

'Police will be coming. Leave her, we'll get her later. We'll ditch the Landrover in Brigstock.'

'We can't leave her. She's a bloody witness. She saw your vehicle. She was supposed to be in bed.'

Marikka froze. She knew that voice. It was the voice that haunted her at night, made her life a misery. None other than her stepfather. So it *had* been him in the Landrover. And she knew he had a sawn off shotgun.

'We're leaving.' The other man repeated, gunning the engine.

She saw the flashlight retreating. A trick? She lay flat in the long grass, holding her breath.

Distant sirens could be heard. Yes, he'd want to get away all right.

'I can see you, Marikka.' His voice was suddenly close. Too close. She looked up momentarily. Saw that he had his shotgun raised.

Deacon suddenly broke away from her. He'd seen him too. Silent and deadly, he ran like lightning towards him, launching himself at her stepfather. The shotgun went off loudly, both barrels. She heard the dog yelp in agony, heard her stepfather fall backwards into the ditch.

The others didn't wait. They drove off back through the woods, spinning wheels. They didn't want to explain anything to the cops.

Marikka ran forward, keeping to the darkest shadows.

Deacon desperately looked up at her, unable to move. The gun had blasted the two of them as the full weight of a ninety-pound Ridgeback forced the short barrel upwards. She couldn't see clearly, but there was a bloody hole where one foreleg had been. He whined as she bent down to caress his head, tears welling in Marikka's eyes.

'Brave boy, my brave, brave, brave boy. Thank you, Deacon.'

Deacon licked her hand, leaving it covered in blood. Then his head abruptly flopped. He was dead. Her heart practically broke in two. Tears flowed now and her throat felt constricted.

Her stepfather lay there inches away. Half his face blown off. The flames from the burning house were reflected in his one remaining glassy eye. His body twitched. He was not quite yet dead. But soon would be. No point in asking why he'd done this. Why he wanted her dead so badly. Her tears weren't for him; that was for sure.

She could see the blue flashing lights on the canal bridge in the distance. The police and fire engines would be here in a few minutes. How could she explain this? Any sensible girl would stay, right? Face the police, and the consequences. But any sensible girl didn't have her firebug record. Or a crazy mother who'd prefer they locked her up and threw away the key. She'd blame her for the fire. She could be really convincing. Probably say she shot her stepfather too.

Well, the only man who could admit guilt for the fire was dead now and so was Deacon. Deacon had saved her life. She'd never forget what he did for her. *Never.*

She glanced back at the house, burning brightly, the flames spreading to nearby trees. They'd never get it put out in time to save anything. That must have been his intention. Probably an insurance scam. Maybe they planned to have her burn with it to make it look like an accident. Maybe that's why her mother had driven off. She was supposed to be dead now. How convenient that would have been for her mother. She could pretend to cry to a whole new audience about the tragic loss of her teen daughter who had so much promise. Yeah right.

She turned on her heels and walked towards the trees. No, she would not be talking to the police. She remembered what those men with her stepfather had said 'We'll get her later.' She wasn't going back to any foster home or 'institution'. She was going to disappear. Change her name back to Stillwater. Set herself free so they couldn't ever find her.

She was already deep into the woods when the first police car finally arrived. She had reached the canal when she saw the flashing lights of the fire engines on the bridge, called in from Brigstock five miles away. They'd save nothing. Find only death and destruction.

She'd stick to the canal. The roads were fraught with danger. She had no doubts about running. She was the type of person who always got blamed for everything. Her head was filled with the last look Deacon had given her. He'd trusted her, loved her, died for her. She felt so sorry. Her heart heavy. Poor Deacon. She wondered how long he'd waited to bite her stepfather. At least he'd had that one opportunity to get his revenge. Her shoulder was giving her pain as her adrenaline rush subsided, it felt strangely hot and sticky. Only now did she remember she'd been shot. There was blood. But there was nothing she could do about it. It would have to wait till morning.

Behind her the sky was bright with the house still burning. It would probably burn for hours. Marikka saw a barge moored by the bridge. She walked by, aware that a man lay snoring on the barge deck, many beer bottles lined up beside him. A banner was loosely hung on the side of the barge reading 'Meet Anya – Discover hidden secrets.'

Marikka tread softly, she didn't want to wake him, suffer any abuse from a drunk.

She didn't notice another pair of sleepless young eyes watching her go by from inside that barge. Curious eyes, who sensed that this girl going by was in big trouble. Vividly she could see traces of her sadness following in her wake, a snake of light that dissolved into the darkness. She would have called out to her, if she could. Told her she was headed the wrong way – that misfortune would certainly find her.

Marikka continued on, unsure where she would go or how she would live. She was sure of only one thing: the canal ended at the sea and that was where she'd make a choice of which way to go. Left or right. Either choice was likely to be wrong, but she was going there anyway.

A shooting star kissed the sky. That's where she was going, she told herself. Wherever it had landed up ahead, that was where she'd go.

TWO

JACKSON & MIKA

Jackson was sitting in the tin bath, half-listening to the radio. It was seven in the morning. He always found it hard to sleep past first light at the best of times; his eyes hurt so much. A near fatal accident and a burning car had left his face looking red raw. It would be months before his skin finally healed. He didn't like to look in the mirror anymore. And it frightened anyone if they ever saw him. He had to wear dark glasses now to see anything properly.

'What was that on the news? I didn't hear it.' He shouted to Mika who was busy making his breakfast in the makeshift kitchen. A simple dirty plastic curtain separated the two spaces.

Mika was the boy, the apprentice, the scruffy long haired runaway who had come to steal food and stayed this past year as his eyes and ears. A wild looking boy with piercing blue eyes. He didn't say much, no doubt resented the early starts and the late evenings, but he didn't complain and seemed to keep himself occupied. Jackson never asked him where he'd come from, or why he was running. He regarded the boy as providence, as something provided, by God, to help him get by. The boy perhaps didn't quite see it that way.

'Mika?'

'They said a big house burned down near Brigstock.'

He sniffed the air. 'You aren't burning the toast, I hope?'

'No.'

'Brigstock, you said? Whose house?'

'A big house. Said the police suspected arson. What's arson?'

'It means someone set the fire deliberately.'

'The Police say they are looking for bodies. They found the owner with his head blown off. Said a dog attacked him.'

Jackson made a face. Didn't seem very likely. Dogs not being well known for their shooting abilities.

'Name?'

'Stander. I think.' Mika always remembered to listen carefully to the early news because he knew he'd be questioned closely. Jackson was very particular about him learning to listen to the details.

Jackson frowned. 'Stander? You sure.'

'Yeah. The police said they are treating it as suspicious.'

'Well, I can't say I'm sorry. He had it coming. I knew him, piece of work that man.'

Jackson climbed out of the tin bath and reached for his towel. He discovered he was tired of living like this. He longed to live somewhere permanent for a while with indoor plumbing. He looked up at the corrugated steel roof with the rusted bolts and sighed. How long had he been here? Too long that was for sure. Time someone else took over and lived on the scraps they gave him.

So Stander was dead. That was interesting. There was a man he wished he'd never met. He had a lot of regrets lately, since the accident.

'I might be going away for a while soon. You be alright living here on your own?'

'Just me?'

'Yes, only you.'

Mika sighed. He didn't mind. He'd grown quite attached to the dunes and the sea. It wasn't much fun here on the reserve, it wasn't close to anything. But it was a home, of sorts. He knew Jackson was strange, but it suited him. He didn't want to be found either.

Jackson appeared fully dressed from behind the curtain, flinging his damp towel to the drying rack and missing it by a mile.

'Honey, toast and coffee. Best way to start the day. You eaten?'

Mika nodded, watching Jackson sit down and feel his way around the table. He couldn't see anything in detail without his glasses.

'Better get started. There's a lot to do, boy.'

Mika nodded. He sighed. There was always a lot to do with the fish. Jackson never tired of giving him things to do.

'Stander,' Jackson muttered to himself. 'I wonder who really shot him?' He sighed. 'Could have been anyone in Brigstock, I suppose. A lot of people will drink to that tonight I'll bet.'

Mika donned his gloves and boots and left Jackson to his ravings. He had work to do. He opened the door and checked the sky. Clear, white fluffy clouds. No rain today then. It almost never rained here.

He grabbed his toolbox and stepped outside.

THREE

RED FLAG

Marikka steadied herself atop the sand dunes and stared with astonishment at the distant shoreline. How was it even possible the tide could go out so far? She could barely see the waves at all. She was exhausted. She'd walked all through the night right the way down the Brigstock Canal. She'd been too scared to sleep anywhere without Deacon beside her. She swayed in the breeze, tired and hungry, wishing she had a better plan. The dunes were singing, the wind in the long grass resonating with a low hum. She'd heard this before, when walking Deacon the previous summer. They had loved the dunes together, the white sand, the utter desolation of it all and here and there the blueberries, blackberries turned blue by the salt air. She ate what she could find and relished the sweet salty tang. It would have to do.

She surveyed the beach, wide and deep with patches of mud showing. Go left and she'd end up in the marshes. Right, she could follow the beach for miles passing the tourist resorts at low tide, stay with the sand all the way to the Point, some thirty or forty miles up the coast. She had no plan beyond that. She'd be safe on the beach in the day, all kinds of people walked their dogs and no one would bother her. She had just enough money for fish and chips in one of the towns, or something, if she got hungry and there were other dunes or golf courses she could hunker down in overnight if need be. But beyond that? Go to London? Isn't that where all the runaway kids ended up? Then what? She knew no one. No one was going to hire her to work. Where to sleep or eat? She wasn't used to living rough. It would be full of freaks and pervs, all too willing to 'help' her if only she'd do something disgusting or illegal and she had no wish to fall into that trap.

She pulled her shirt away from her shoulder to examine her wound. Just a graze, it was already forming a scab, but a lot of blood had seeped into her sleeve and around her neck. She'd survive. Couldn't believe he'd so calmly shoot her like that. She knew he hated her, the very first day she'd met him, but not enough to shoot her, or burn her alive.

She just had to sleep. Luckily the dunes were deserted. Few people came here anyway. The only road stopped a few miles back and only hikers and dog lovers knew it, she recalled, as she spotted another berry bush. She noticed a ragged red flag flying from a pole in the distance. Wondered why it was up? Surely no one would be swimming with the tide so far out. Couldn't think why anyone would put up a warning flag out here and figured they must have forgotten it and left it flying.

She found a deep hollow, well sheltered from the wind and curled up to sleep. She'd be safe enough in the day, she hoped. She looked around for Deacon. Felt a stab of pain to accept, once again, that he wasn't there to protect her. She felt very vulnerable without him nuzzling closely, his quizzical eyebrows always checking on her to make sure she was safe.

In moments she was fast asleep, lulled by the humming of the dunes.

She didn't hear the first jet. She felt the second as the ground shook under her. She'd been dreaming about her mother when sand suddenly covered her face and she woke up startled, momentarily disorientated. She heard the jet as it flashed overhead, no more than a hundred feet above her. She stood up bewildered, still half-way between a deep sleep and this terrifying moment. She climbed to the top of the dune and saw another fighter jet coming in fast, aiming for a red flare burning on the beach. She saw it drop something and miss, the object bouncing at an incredible speed towards the dunes.

She must have screamed as she jumped back down. The impact of the explosion sent sand and bushes flying everywhere. She closed her eyes and rolled up in a tight ball as the jet flew right overhead, even lower than the last. Her heart was beating so fast she thought she'd be sick. She didn't wait for another jet to appear. She picked herself up and ran inland, following the path in the dunes to god knows where, but anywhere but here.

A root snagged her foot and she fell headlong and rolled down into a dip coming face to face with a faded signpost.

WARNING: Fleet Dunes and Tidal Beaches
This is a restricted area. When the Red Flag is flying this area is off limits to the public. The beach and dunes are all within target range. Strict observation of this regulation must be observed. No person should be seaward of this sign.
Ministry of Defence

Target range? The MOD were allowed to bomb the beach and the dunes?

Marikka lay prostrate on the sand unable to believe what she was reading. But a dim memory of something her stepfather had told her about the dunes was coming back. As a child he'd watched the RAF flying from here. There was an old airbase nearby, left over from the war. Gone now. But they still returned to practice bombing and the area was still controlled by the MOD.

Marikka gathered herself and moved to the other side of the sign, thoroughly awake now. No wonder there weren't any other walkers out here. She could have been killed and she'd even seen the red flag flying. She had no excuse.

Another jet roared overhead, but she didn't even look up this time. She grimaced to herself, hearing Felicity's voice, a girl from school that she played tennis with on Saturdays. 'You have to be the unluckiest girl in the world, Marikka. Nothing ever goes right for you.'

Felicity would laugh if she told her she'd nearly been blown up, right after nearly being burned to death in her own home. She'd say 'Things go in threes Marikka. You want to watch out for the next one, try to see it coming and duck.'

Yes. There would be a lot of bad luck to come, she sensed with a bitter smile. Might even have been better if the bomb *had* dropped on her head.

She stayed exactly where she was for a good half hour. Her great theory was that they wouldn't bomb the warning sign. Stood to reason. This *had* to be the safest place to be.

She stood, shook all the sand out of her hair and clothes. She was thirsty and wondered if it was safe to drink the water in the marshes, doubted it. But if she could find a stream it might be OK to drink from it. Deacon drank from the streams all the time and it never affected him.

A shadow passed over her, she looked up in time to see a sparrow-hawk glide on by, its eyes ever on the lookout for a small bird or rodent it could snatch and eat. It didn't seem to be affected by the jets at all.

She moved back up to the adjacent dune and surveyed the beach. The flare was nearly extinguished, small wisps of smoke drifting along the sand. She couldn't see any damage. Perhaps the explosions were small. After all it was only practice.

The sky was clear. She looked back down the dunes and saw the red flag was gone. Almost as if it had never existed. Time to move on.

She turned and headed over the dunes again to the beach, stopping only to remove her sneakers and carry them draped around her shoulders. It was good to feel the cold sand against her bare feet, the wind blew her long, untamed hair behind her.

'Deacon!' She shouted. As if shouting his name would bring him back to her.

Walking without him was ridiculous. Nothing felt right. She forced herself not to think about her mother and her parting words of accusation. She realised there was probably some kind of police hunt for the girl who burned down the family home.

She'd walked maybe four or five miles along the beach now. Something tugged at her memory. She remembered she'd been near here a year before with Monday, her horse. Got yelled at because this beach area was off limits. She had no idea why the MOD could own such a beautiful stretch of sand. The seaside resort of Scarness would be some twenty miles from where she stood. What was so special about this bit of beach? Why did they have to own it or bomb it? Had to be places that weren't so beautiful they could bomb, surely.

She smiled briefly recalling how much Monday had loved the firm sand underfoot and enjoyed bathing in the salt water. All Mr Cole's doing, the amazing patient vet who'd treated him. Monday had been all on his toes, becoming impossible. He'd made her bring him down to the beach and run him off the bridle, let him have his head. Once in the salt water it was hard to get him out, even with the waves coming at him, but it had done the trick. That horse finally understood what happiness was. He returned home a different animal and then her damn stepfather had turned around and sold him. Just like that.

She thought about sending a letter. Explain how her stepfather caused the fire and shot Deacon. Tell the police she was running because she couldn't trust anyone, especially social services. Then swore, who'd believe her anyway. Dumb.

She felt so alone without Deacon at her side; it felt wrong, unnatural. She tried to suppress a sudden surge of anger at her situation. First her mother accused her of burning the house down, then her stepfather tries to kill her. Best to be numb. If she felt anything at all she'd probably crumple up and cry and crying wasn't going to help. She could still see the hatred on her mother's face as she wound down the car window to scream at her. *Please god, never let me be like her, never let me hate anyone as much as she hates me*

FOUR

FLOWERS

The flowers began to gather later that day. People didn't know where to put them, considering the house had burned down. They left them just outside the police cordon tape at the driveway's end. They, like many others, that came to gawp, stared in fascination at the smoking ruins, watching the last of the exhausted firemen as they tried to dampen down the smoldering ruins. Over twenty blackened tree trunks stood vigil over the remains.

'For Slim – we will all miss you.' The hastily scrawled notes declared.

Soon more flowers appeared with sad messages for Marikka, aka Slim. Two red-eyed sniveling girls arrived to pay their respects and stare at the ruins and leave messages tied to the gatepost. They didn't stay long and ran back to their waiting mother in her Volvo Estate.

All told there were twenty-four personal messages for her. Had she seen them, she would have been surprised that there were any at all.

Most village folk weren't at all surprised that Stander had been shot. There were plenty who would have supplied their own shotgun to the dog that allegedly did it. They'd all heard the rumour that it was arson; more than a few knew Stander was late on his bills, in trouble with the taxman and short of money. Speculation flew about who had done it and the whereabouts of Marikka's mother, seen by no one. The police were talking murder, according to some gossipers. Even now some cops wearing protective HAZMAT gear were sifting through the ashes, trying to put together what had happened.

Somehow, and this raised some curiosity, they hadn't yet discovered evidence of any bodies. But then again, it had been a very fierce fire and so much had disappeared in the flames. It was a one-day wonder in Brigstock. Gossip would move on.

FIVE

CRASH

The car came racing out from between the dunes and the driver was heading straight out to sea. She was about to enjoy seeing the vehicle crash into the waves when it suddenly accelerated, turning sharply, causing a mini tidal wave of spray as it skidded around to face the dunes again, racing away from the waves with a roar from its engine, wheels spinning in the wet sand. The driver had to have seen her. She was the only one on the beach for miles.

The car was approaching the dunes stupidly fast and she was beginning to wonder how it was going to stop when all four wheels locked up as it tried to brake. The driver had hit a shallow stretch of water and was aquaplaning at full tilt, heading in a straight line right for the dunes. It was going to crash. The driver would be killed for certain. She watched with astonishment as it ploughed headfirst into the sand dune, a terrible graunching noise sounded as metal and sand met at speed. She was already running after it as a huge shower of sand went skywards.

The driver had to be dead. He had to be.

She ran as fast as she could, her shoes banging against her chest. She couldn't believe that she'd witnessed this.

The car was almost completely buried into the dune. The only way to get the driver out would be through the rear hatch. She arrived breathless, scared as to what she would find.

She dumped her shoes in the sand, opened up the hatch and to her utmost surprise heard laughing. A Kid with long scraggly hair and sun-burnished skin was in the driver's seat laughing. The kind of laugh you make when you're surprised you survived something utterly stupid. Like driving a car at ninety miles an hour into the middle of a sand dune.

'Oh my God. I can't believe you're actually alive.'

The kid stopped laughing. He couldn't move. He was pinned into his seat by the airbag.

'Don't move,' Marikka instructed him. 'You'll have to come out the back way. Are you all right?'

Mika had no idea where the girl had come from, but he was glad there was someone there. He'd definitely braked way too late.

'Lower your right hand. The lever to lower the seat back is on your right, I think.'

Mika reluctantly sought the lever and pulled it up, instantly discovering his arms hurt like hell. The seat reclined and he was able to wiggle free of the airbag. That's when the leg pain kicked in.

'Ow... Ow.' He had sudden shooting pains in both legs. 'Bloody hell. OW.'

'You probably jarred your legs. Take your time. Don't rush. Can you start to slide back? I'll pull you.'

Mika felt arms sliding around him as the girl began to pull him away from the seat and the airbag. His legs hurt like hell. And what had he done to his arms?

'I'm OK. I'm OK.' He was saying, but she kept on pulling him gently out and he heard her take a sharp intake of breath when she saw the blood.

'You're bleeding. Can you feel your toes? Wiggle your feet if you can.'

Mika wiggled his feet and saw them move, but the pain was even more intense now and he winced, eyes smarting with pain.

He said nothing more, not quite so brave anymore, worried about the damage. Jackson wouldn't be kind. He was always telling him to be careful.

'This is the tricky bit. Got to get you over the lip. Don't know why they don't make them flat. Can you turn your body maybe?'

Mika saw her for the first time. Surprised at how young she was, how beautiful, if you liked freckles and red hair...

Marikka stared as this boy, astonished all over again at how young he was. No more than fourteen if a day. What was he doing driving cars? Couldn't be legal. He was so brown and his wild long hair bleached almost white by the sun. He had fair eyebrows and a pretty nose… She quickly stopped staring at him and concentrated on his injuries.

'Don't move quickly. You've got two deep gashes in your legs, your right arm is injured too. Don't move, OK? You must have broken some bones.'

Mika blinked. His whole body was convulsed by pain now. It was rolling over him in waves and he was suddenly short of breath.

Marikka swung his legs around so he could place them outside the car and now in the glare of the sun she could see his injuries more clearly. He'd need surgery, stitches at the very least.

Mika looked at his wounds and suddenly felt dizzy. Jackson, he realised, wouldn't like this. He'd have to go to hospital and they'd ask awkward questions. He had no identification or numbers… some busybody would call social services. He didn't want that.

'We need to staunch the bleeding. I need a first-aid kit.'

Mika was definitely feeling woozy now, remembering suddenly that he'd banged his head hard against the headrest.

'Back of the dunes. There's an old RAF hangar. But you can't go in…'

Mika suddenly slumped back unconscious.

Marikka took a deep breath and slowly hauled him out. They were about equal in height and weight.

She staggered as his dead weight pressed down on her and she laid him down slowly beside the car, deftly dragging some matting from the car to put under his legs to reduce the amount of sand that would get into the wounds.

'I'm going to get help,' she told him, even knowing he was unconscious. 'Don't move.'

As Marikka climbed the huge dune she slowly became aware that the whole area was strewn with rubbish. Whoever this kid was he'd turned the nature reserve into a scrap heap. She was appalled. How had he been allowed to get away with this?

On the other side of the dune she found one giant Nissen hangar made out of corrugated steel and painted black. The boy lived in this? All around it were various broken cars, rusting metal and one large green ancient bus. Whoever they were, they had ruined the reserve.

SIX

FIRST AID

Jackson was cleaning the water testing equipment when he heard the knock on the door. Normally he'd ignore anyone knocking. Mika would answer it, or else they'd go away after a while.

The knocking continued.

'Hello? I need help here. A boy is hurt.' It was a young girl's voice if he wasn't mistaken.

A boy? A young boy? Mika? He began to frown.

Reluctantly Jackson made his way to the door (collecting a stick for his defence on the way) and unlocked it, opening it just an inch.

'There's a boy hurt,' Marikka told him breathlessly. 'He says he lives here. He crashed a car and he's bleeding. He passed out.' Marikka nervously stepped back a little at the sight of the very strange man with a large stick who had opened the door. He was tall with a mop of untidy white hair with clear signs of his face having been burned, his eyebrows were missing and his skin was shiny red raw in places. He wore thick tinted glasses and she could see his hands were bandaged.

'I need a first aid kit and …' her voice trailed away. She wanted to run away, this man looked truly scary.

Jackson was surprised that the girl seemed quite genuinely concerned about Mika.

'I believe it's on the shelving in what we mockingly call the kitchen. To my right.' He stepped aside and let her in. He stayed exactly where he was as he listened to her make her way to the makeshift kitchen. He heard her hesitation as she looked around, sensed her shock at the primitive conditions he lived in, heard her fumble around the shelves to find what she'd come for.

Anxious to get back to the boy Marikka returned, pausing

uncertainly at the door.

'I've taken some bandages and some antiseptic as well. He needs an ambulance. Can you call for one?'

Jackson stared down at her with hostile piercing eyes, making Marikka feel extremely uncomfortable.

'It's his own fault. I told him not to drive so fast. Boy's got to learn his lesson.'

Marikka spluttered a protest.

'Lesson? His legs are bleeding. He's got concussion. He might have brain damage.'

Jackson pursed his lips as if he doubted her words. 'You're the Doctor,' he told her sarcastically and slammed the door in her face.

Marikka couldn't believe it. He wouldn't phone for an ambulance? Was the man crazy?

She ran back to the boy wondering what the hell she had stumbled on. A lesson, this was a lesson?

Jackson stood behind the closed door still frowning. Only now did he wonder where she'd come from. He shrugged. She'd bring the boy home. He'd heard the car impacting the dune. He'd thought at the time that Mika was driving too fast. Well, he'd learn something today. Something he'd remember no doubt the next time he went out in a car. He wondered how bad his injuries really were? One thing was for sure, there was no way the boy could go to the hospital. Not ever. No one knew that boy was here and he didn't want any awkward questions.

Marikka had done her best to clean and dress his wounds before he stirred, unable to stop the sand from getting everywhere. She hadn't stopped the bleeding, the wounds would definitely have to be stitched. He was lucky not to have severed any arteries.

Mika tried to sit up, but felt incredibly dizzy. He remembered the airbag had hit his head with such force against the headrest.

'Who are you?' he asked weakly, rubbing his sore head.

Marikka smiled as she packed away the kit and closed the box. 'Slim. I mean, Marikka. Don't make any sudden movements, you've banged your head and everything else.'

Mika felt the back of his head, found a rapidly rising bruise. He didn't know where this girl had come from, he virtually never saw anyone from day to day.

'Mag what?' He asked.

'Marikka. You?'

'Mika.' He mumbled. 'My legs.' The pain was growing in strength as feeling came back into them and made him feel even more dizzy.

'Mika, like in Finnish?' Marikka asked. She wanted him to talk, she could see he was close to passing out again.

Mika nodded.

'Why were you driving so fast?' She asked him. 'I don't understand what's going on here, but I know an idiot when I see one. Don't you have brakes?'

Mika shook his head. 'Aquaplaned. They wouldn't work.'

Marikka squatted on her haunches and examined the boy's head.

'We really have to get you to hospital.'

'Jackson won't let me go.' Mika asserted. He was sure of that.

'Nonsense. You'll get an infection if your legs aren't treated. You need x-rays. You've got concussion.'

Mika shrugged. He knew Jackson. He was surprised he'd even let her have the first aid kit.

'I have to get you back to the … whatever it is you live in.'

'It's a blister hangar. Bombers flew out from here right across the beach to Germany in the war.'

'This is supposed to be a nature reserve. For birds and stuff, not you, or the bombers.'

Mika didn't know why she was so angry.

'Help me up?' he asked.

Mika held out her hands to him and he gripped them tight. An electric spark snapped loudly between them and they both let go momentarily shouting out with the shock.

'Wow … did you feel that?' Marikka exclaimed.

Mika's hand still tingled. That had never happened before, his whole body seemed electrically charged. He nervously touched one finger to Marikka's hand and this time there was no shock. She gripped both of his hands again and pulled him up, steadying him on his feet.

Mika felt the rush of blood through his legs and the pain intensified. He did his best to ignore it, but Marikka could see he was hurting and grinding his teeth together with the effort of standing.

'Put your good arm around me and let me take your weight, all right? Come on, let's get you some help.'

Mika gingerly began to walk, wincing with every step.

'Is that your father down there in the hut thing?' Marikka asked.

'No.' Mika answered. He didn't want to tell her anything more. He fished in his pocket and pulled out a pretty silver object. He gave it to Marikka who looked at him puzzled.

'Got nothin' else.' He said.

Marikka glanced at the object; it looked old and valuable. She could pawn it if she needed cash later. She pocketed it, straining to keep them both upright as they walked up the dune. She wondered what the hell she was getting into and who the weirdo with the burns was. Something wasn't right here, that was for sure.

A seagull shrieked at them from a safe distance as clouds began to gather over the sea.

SEVEN

NORMALLY I TREAT POODLES

Mika had protested when she had suggested seeing the vet, Mr Cole, but Jackson had point blank refused to have him taken to hospital, what with all the questions they'd ask about the boy. That was the trouble with runaways he'd said. They invited all kinds of intrusions and prying eyes from officials, he wasn't going to permit it. Marikka was so angry she almost washed her hands of both of them, but she knew she couldn't abandon Mika.

She put him on a cart attached to an old rattle trap bicycle outside the hut and peddled furiously all the way to Huddlebank, outside the MOD zone, in the hope that the vet wouldn't turn them away.

Mr Cole, older and smaller than she remembered, had looked at Marikka with total surprise and confusion and stared uselessly at the unconscious Mika in open-mouthed astonishment.

'I'm just amazed to see you're alive, Marikka. I heard about the fire and the shooting on the radio. I thought you were dead. I really did. I've been upset all morning about it.'

Marikka, breathless and exhausted from the ride on a difficult muddy track, stood swaying on his doorstep. 'I promised to help this boy, Mr Cole. He's bleeding and...'

Mr Cole seeing her obvious distress bent down to examine the boy. Saw the blood pooling under the boy's legs and pulled a face. Clearly she wanted him to deal with it.

'We'll stop the bleeding and then perhaps call an ambulance, all right? You've grown taller. Must be almost a year since I saw you last.'

Marikka didn't answer, she was concerned only with saving Mika, not any chit-chat. They carried Mika through the waiting room to his stainless steel surgery table, jumping ahead of an impatient woman with a constipated poodle, much to her obvious irritation. They laid Mika out there on the polished metal surface.

Mr Cole expertly cleaned the wounds and stitched him up, eyeing Marikka as he sewed. She squirmed, knew he'd be asking lots of awkward questions. She was dreading it. She looked at the small man with delicate hands and grey hair and thought back to how kind he'd been to her the year before. She'd not really met many kind people. It was him who'd made her bring her horse Monday down to the beach for a week to exercise him in the salt water and strengthen his calves. It worked. Monday loved riding in the spray and the wide-open expanse of the sands at low tide. One had to be careful of soft sand and niggling holes, but Monday had taken it in his stride. Never was a horse more sad to leave the beach than Monday.

Mr Cole looked at her with a twinkle in his eyes. 'I normally treat poodles. Makes a change, eh? Boy's not likely to bite do y'think?'

Marikka understood he was trying to amuse her, but she didn't feel right, heard her stomach growl and remembered that she hadn't eaten much besides the berries earlier.

'So Monday is gone?' Mr Cole asked, as he cut the thread on the first leg.

Marikka nodded. 'My stepfather sold him. Said he couldn't afford to feed me *and* a horse. I had to choose.'

Mr Cole nodded gravely. 'Knowing you, you offered to stop eating.'

Marikka smiled briefly. 'He was tempted, I know that. But he'd already sold him. Went to Daniella West. She's got a great big field for him to kick around in.'

Mr Cole snatched another look at her. 'I'm glad to hear it. This boy of yours is going to have some nasty scars, you know that, of course.' He sighed. 'Aye, the hospital would make a neater job of it than me.'

'I'm just grateful you'd do it.'

'Car accident you said?'

'His foot slipped on the pedal, or something. Big bang.'

'This little lad was the driver?' Mr Cole asked surprised.

Marikka realised she'd made a mistake. Too late to retract it now.

'These gashes are nasty. Luckily missed his nerves, you cleaned him up well. Who is he?'

'Just a boy.'

Mr Cole pursed his lips. 'Just a boy? The truth please, Marikka.'

Marikka watched fascinated as he stitched Mika's other leg, blood still oozing over the table.

'He's helping out someone on the nature reserve. Work experience, he said. I don't think they wanted to get in trouble since he was driving. You know how social services can be. It was his fault anyway, drove too fast.'

'That I can tell. What the hell did he hit?'

Marikka didn't answer. Mika was slowly coming around, but not yet talking. Marikka wondered if he could feel his legs being stitched like that. Had to hurt with needles going into his flesh.

'Isn't it terrible about Mollie Pendleton? It's not worth being rich these days. They snatched the child right outside her school. Police say that they're awaiting news of a ransom.'

Marikka looked blank. She'd never heard of any kid called Mollie.

'The Pendleton's own the pig farm outside Brigstock. Tricky beasts to keep healthy, pigs. I hope they don't harm the child. Rumour of a kidnap gang operating in these parts – but that's just gossip I suppose. Mind you they said you were dead on the radio this morning. Seems you can't trust what you hear on the news at all. It's a terrible thing to lose your stepfather like that. And shot by a dog. Your dog Deacon I suspect. How likely is that?' He looked directly at Marikka for confirmation and she looked away. She had no idea what the news was saying, but she was surprised to hear she was supposed to be dead.

Mika opened his eyes. He'd heard and looked at Marikka with surprise.

'Ow.' He wriggled on the table.

'Keep still, young man. I'm nearly done. These are nasty wounds.'

Mika winced as he looked at Marikka. 'It was your house that burned? It was on the radio.'

'Deacon didn't kill my stepfather. He was trying to shoot Deacon and me... He was defending me.'

Mr Cole raised an eyebrow. 'Why on earth would your stepfather want to kill you, or the dog?'

'It was arson,' Mika chipped in, proud he'd remembered that word. 'They said it was arson. You finished? That hurts.'

Marikka looked out of the window a moment. She wondered if Mr Cole would call the police. She wanted to run away, but stood there like dummy. She'd promised to get Mika home and hated to break a promise.

'My stepfather and his friends came home with some cans of petrol and well, you know the rest.' Marikka didn't want to discuss it.

Mr Cole glanced at Marikka again, realising for the first time that her right shoulder was covered in dried blood.

'What happened to your shoulder, Marikka?'

She had forgotten about that in all the fuss.

'It must be Mika's blood,' she said, none too convincingly.

Mr Cole attended to the last stitches. 'Stay still, my boy. You're going to be extremely sore a few days. Keep the cuts bandaged for at least three days if you can. No showers or baths.'

Mika wasn't listening, trying to see what had happened to his legs.

'I don't think he washes much anyway,' Marikka said with a sly grin. 'He's a boy.'

Mr Cole smiled. 'Well I don't want any infection to get in there. Normally I keep a dog in overnight with wounds like this.'

'I'm no dog,' Mika protested, suddenly taking an interest.

Mr Cole cut the other thread and began to clean the blood around the wounds.

'Was it a wall you went into?'

'Concrete,' Mika answered, too quickly

'Well, I'd say the concrete won. You've got major bruising and discolouration forming. You've jarred both legs and that right arm too. You'll be a mass of purple bruises by tonight. Watch out for sore hips as well. Rest. Understand? I know young boys hate to lie still, but rest, or you'll regret it.'

He handed Mika a small glass of water and some pills. 'Painkillers. I'm going to give some to Marikka to administer to you, but no more than six in a day. Is that clear?' He turned to Marikka. 'Six only; spaced over a few hours between. Understood? No matter if he asks for more. Make him have plenty to drink and try not to move him. Rest, rest, rest is what he needs.'

Mr Cole stood up to straighten his back, then abruptly pulled at the bloodied t-shirt covering Marikka's shoulder. He could see it was red raw, saw the shot had only grazed her, but would leave her a scar. He looked her in the eyes. 'You were telling the truth. I'll have to clean that up as well.'

Marikka wished she'd never come here now. Everything was going to go wrong. She'd hardly gone far on her big escape. He'd want her to surrender herself. Probably thought she'd set the damn fire. She wondered when her mother would be on the news. She wouldn't be able to resist being on the news to slag her wicked daughter off.

'I'm not going back home, Mr Cole.'

Mr Cole turned to her and began to clean the wound.

'I'm not judging you, Marikka. Just tell me the truth whilst I clean this up, or do you want it to get septic?'

Marikka stood there patiently as he disinfected the wound. Mika was staring at her in wonder with his bright blue eyes.

'I didn't do anything. I was just lucky. I had a headache and went to bed without supper…' she began. She told him everything. How Deacon had been tied up. How she'd gone all the way back in to the burning house to save her mother, only to have her scream abuse at her and blame her for the fire. It was almost a relief to share it with them and hear herself say it all. It was ridiculous, stupid and she knew she was being foolish running away once she actually explained everything, but it had made sense at the time.

Mr Cole smoothed some anti-septic on the wound and placed a large bandage over it. 'It will be sore for a couple of days, but you were lucky. Very lucky.' He sat down, exhausted, aware that there was still a dog in the waiting room.

'I don't understand why he'd set his own house on fire,' Mr Cole added.

'He owed money to the taxman. A lot of money.' Marikka explained. 'He didn't want them to get a penny.'

'Did you happen to see the numberplate on the Landrover the men were driving?'

Marikka screwed up her eyes to try and remember. She could see the vehicle disappearing into the woods with her father in the back seat. 'Y L 63. I don't remember it all. Except it was red, dark red.'

Mr Cole wrote the number and colour down on his pad. 'Then you'll permit me to tell the police this much.'

'They'll want to know how you know.'

'I'll tell them I had walkers through here this morning. They told me about the fire. They could have told me about the Landrover.'

Mika was thinking that Mr Cole must like this girl a lot, if he was prepared to lie for her.

'It's plausible,' Marikka granted. 'So you won't tell them I was here?'

'I know what you went through at home, Marikka. I couldn't really say anything, but he was a cruel man and your mother not much better. Go. Take the boy home.'

Marikka took out the silver broach that Mika had given her. Mika looked pained that she had so quickly given it away.

'It's all we have,' Marikka explained, avoiding Mika's eyes.

Mr Cole took the object, putting it up to the light to examine it and the indentations on the base. 'Pretty. Solid silver too. Consider the bill paid.' He looked at Marikka with some concern.

'You have somewhere to go?'

Mika stood uncertainly, testing his stitches and whether he could actually walk. He was nervous and sore as the painkillers hadn't done their work yet.

'She's with me now,' he told Mr Cole; frowning as he tried to bend his legs. 'It's real tight. You sure that's right?'

'It's supposed to be tight, what you think holds all the blood in? Don't put pressure on them. How are you getting him home, Marikka?'

'I've got the little trailer and a bike.'

Mr Cole shook his head, bemused, looking at Mika.

'Well all I can say is avoid any concrete walls. You should be in a hospital, my boy. I can still call an ambulance for you.'

Mika shook his head. 'No hospitals. Not ever going to a hospital.'

Mr Cole shrugged. He didn't want to force the issue.

Marikka swayed, her stomach grumbling again.

'You eaten anything lately?' Mr Cole asked her seeing her eyes flutter. He realized she needed food.

Marikka shrugged. 'Some berries…'

He pointed. 'My kitchen, now. You know where it is. You're in shock. My fault. I should have thought of that. Go in there, find yourself something and make me some tea whilst you are at it. No sugar, just milk. I've got a worried dog out there to deal with.'

Marikka took a deep breath and grabbed Mika by the arm and headed towards the inner door. Mika walked slowly, wincing with each step.

'Don't make a mess,' he added as he turned away.

'Thank you, Mr Cole.'

'No mess,' he repeated.

Marikka opened the door to find they were in a dark corridor leading to another door, the kitchen.

Inside the very tidy kitchen she sat Mika down at the table and set about finding bread and jam and boiling water in the kettle. There was a good view of the road and the dunes from here. Mr Cole could walk from the house to the sea from his back garden, how neat was that?

'My legs hurt. My arm too.' Mika complained, trying to move his arm.

'He gave you a tetanus shot, to be sure. They always hurt. Said you were really lucky not to break anything. Although I still say you need an x-ray. Raspberry or dark honey?'

Mika frowned. He wasn't feeling good, but toast and jam sounded good. 'Raspberry. No tea. He got milk? Milk at the hangar always goes off.'

Marikka opened the fridge. 'Yep. Lots of milk.' She poured them both a glass and she drank hers quickly discovering how thirsty she was.

'Can you trust him?' Mika asked, as they waited for the kettle to boil.

Marikka nodded. 'He came when Monday was sick and stayed all night with him in the stable. He was an Army vet. Been everywhere. He told me tons of stories of him in Iraq in the first Gulf war.'

'I can't believe your own father shot you.'

'Stepfather.'

Mika lifted his shirt to reveal a huge scar on his back. 'My father's present on my thirteenth birthday. I spilled some paint. I don't remember much, but I was in hospital for a month. One day they said he was coming to get me to take me home and I just ran. Been running ever since. A year now.' He suddenly grinned. 'Jackson's weird, but never asks me about it.'

Marikka was spreading jam on toast, nibbling on another hot slice as she did so. She was starving.

'Jackson will have to let you stay. I can't do my job now.' Mika looked down at his legs and could barely move them he was so sore. 'You could help out, until I'm better. He'll see that makes sense. You don't have to stay like, forever, just until I'm moving again. A week maybe. At least you'll have somewhere to sleep. Toilet's in the bushes but …'

Marikka grimaced. 'The bushes? You really know how to impress a girl, eh?'

'I dug a hole. We just put lime on it and then I dig another hole. It's what you're supposed to do.'

'And my duties?' Marikka asked. 'Aside from wrecking cars and abandoning them on the dunes.'

Mika frowned, annoyed at being teased.

'You have to stay. He's going to leave soon anyway.'

'I'm not sure. Jackson's weird and I don't like the mess you guys have made of the reserve.'

'We're the other side of the sign. It's not the reserve there. Besides, we didn't cause the mess. Jackson says those cars have been there years.

'Doesn't matter. It's supposed to be for the birds and animals, not you, or him.'

'You have to help. I'll feed you. I do all the cooking.'

'Do you ever wash your hands first?' Marikka asked, looking at his blackened nails.

Mika looked at his hands and the mixture of blood and oil.

'I wash in the sea all the time. Salt kills everything.'

'Soap works too, I hear.'

Mika didn't know what else to say. He didn't really want to admit that he wanted her to stay, that he was lonely and needed a friend, someone to talk to. She wasn't like any other girl he'd ever met. She was … different.

'So are you going to explain what it is you and Jackson are doing there at the hanger? Or do I have to guess?' Marikka asked, as she passed him a round of toast and jam whilst she made two cups of tea. 'Wait. I'm taking the tea to Mr Cole. Don't move.'

Marikka grabbed the mug and disappeared back the way they had come.

Mika stayed put looking over the kitchen. It was old fashioned, but homely. Been a long time since he'd been in a clean and organised home. He looked down at his thighs and wondered how bad the scarring would be. Looked really scary right now and he could see his skin was already turning purple where he'd been bruised.

Marikka returned and he heard a dog yapping in the surgery behind her.

'I couldn't do that job,' she said making a face. 'Dogs bite when they're distressed.'

Marikka picked up her tea and sighed. She'd have to go with the boy for now. Common sense told her that she should get away, but another set of senses told her that having an actual place to stay over for a week was sensible too and the boy would certainly need help in whatever he did.

'So tell me about Jackson, Mika. You're both living like cavemen for a reason. What is it? And the burns?' Marikka asked. 'He's pretty scary looking.'

Mika didn't want to answer and then noticed there was a blue flashing light outside the window. He shouted. 'Shit. Police. The police are here! The vet must have called them.'

Marikka saw the flashing lights and instantly ran for the back door, looking back at Mika who shuffled after her, wincing with every step.

A moment later the kitchen door opened and Mr Cole stood there, looking at the abandoned toast and mug of tea. He sighed. He spoke to the empty room.

'I was coming to warn you the police have brought in an injured dog.'

He surveyed the mess, picked up a slice of buttered toast and ate it. He wished she hadn't run, it was the last thing he wanted.

Marikka and Mika were in the dunes peering back from behind the cover of a bramble bush.

'I can't believe he called the cops,' Marikka was saying, the disappointment in her voice hard to hide.

Mika was watching the cop car carefully, regretting the walk up the dune with his sore legs. His eyes were wet with the pain. Worse he was beginning to realise that they'd run for no good reason.

'I don't think... look. They're carrying a dog out of the car.'

Deacon? Marikka suddenly thought, then just as quickly dismissed the thought. Deacon was long gone.

They had left too hastily. It was entirely logical that the cops would bring an injured dog to a vet. But then again, if the cops had seen them they might have asked awkward questions.

She felt foolish now. But it was too late to go back, too embarrassing.

'Come on, let's get the bike. Can you walk?'

Mika stood awkwardly. 'Give me your arm. I swear he sewed me up too tight. It hurts. It really hurts.'

She could see his eyes were watering. It had to hurt.

'Take my arm. You have to lie down.'

Mika gripped her arm hard as they slid down the dune.

'He likes you.'

'Who?'

'The vet. I could tell. You really had a horse?'

Marikka nodded. 'Yeah. Monday was special. But he was never really happy on his feet until Mr Cole came along. He's really good with animals.'

They stopped by the bike and he lay down on the trailer, relieved to take the pressure off his stitches. The cops inside the surgery were paying them no attention at all.

'Hang on,' Marikka told him as she pedalled away.

EIGHT

A DEAD MAN

He sat in the chair, pale, unshaven, exhausted, hardly able to comprehend what the detective was telling him. It was 10.30 in the morning. He'd come up from London the moment he'd heard the news and Detective Barber wasn't being very cooperative.

'You say you haven't seen your daughter in four years?' He was sceptical, examining the man's diving licence and passport brought for identification.

'Longer. I last saw her when she was turning nine. Her mother was given custody. Fathers have no rights apparently.'

The detective put a hand through his short greying hair and tried to look sympathetic. He knew enough men like him who were denied access to their kids by the courts and a vindictive wife. Then again, it didn't mean he was innocent.

'And you had no access at all?'

'I was granted access. She was supposed to come to me on weekends. My wife took off before I returned.'

The detective frowned and looked at the report he'd been sent about Marikka.

'Your daughter was in several foster homes for three years before coming to live here. I don't understand...'

Leon Stillwater looked surprised by that and hurt. 'Foster homes? No, that's impossible. When? She was...' He stared uncomprehending at the detective. 'It cost me everything to try and prevent her from keeping Marikka. She lied through her teeth to the courts to keep her. Marikka couldn't have been fostered.'

The detective raised an eyebrow. The records were correct. 'According to these records your daughter was also cautioned when she was nine after burning down a garden shed. Social services were involved and they provided her a secure foster home.'

This was news to Leon Stillwater. 'But why wasn't I informed?'

The detective looked at him more closely. Mr Stillwater didn't look well. Exhausted even.

'To be frank, sir, I don't think they were even told of your existence. According to statements here you were listed as deceased so...'

Leon looked up sharply. 'Clearly that isn't true.'

'It would seem your daughter was told that you died...'

'I was in Italy, on business. I had a car accident. Hit and run ...'

'And when you returned you made no attempt to contact your ex-wife or your daughter?'

Leon nearly exploded he was so angry about this.

'I had to re-learn how to walk; my spine was damaged. After four months in traction in Milan I returned to discover my wife had completely vanished. I assumed she had Marikka with her. I couldn't find any trace. She'd changed surnames, forged my signature and sold the house. Half that £450,000 she got for it was mine. I have been searching for Marikka for six years, Detective Barber. You have no idea what it is like to totally lose contact with your daughter like that, to have her snatched away. And now you tell me she was fostered?'

The detective made a face. It was a tragedy, but not his department.

'I'm sorry, but you have no idea how evil her mother is,' Leon continued. 'I only came up here because when I heard a child called Marikka had died I thought there might be a small chance it was her. I didn't want to believe she was dead, but just ....' exasperated he ran out of words.

The Detective looked at another report. 'Your ex-wife has made a telephone report blaming the fire on your daughter. We have tried to contact her this morning to make a statement but she has disappeared.'

Leon buried his face in his hands. He despaired.

'More games. Of course she's gone. She's in breach of a court order and stolen money. She's an evil woman, detective. Nothing she says can be trusted. Why on earth would my daughter burn her home down?'

The detective held up his hand. 'I never get involved in domestics. But the accusation has been made and we will be investigating. And I have to tell you that we aren't certain that she perished in the fire.'

Leon looked up, confused. 'The news said…'

'Our forensic team are still working on the site and haven't yet found any …'

The detective didn't really want to continue. He didn't want to give this distraught man false hope. 'Then there's this business of her burning down a shed.'

'I know nothing about that and you said she was nine when that happened?'

The detective held up his hand. 'We explore all avenues, sir. I'm just saying, until evidence of her is found in the ashes, we can't be sure of anything. There could be another reason why they haven't found anything. She may have been away with friends. Might still be away. We're making enquiries.'

Leon allowed himself a surge of hope. Marikka was alive. 'Perhaps she was on a sleepover?'

'Maybe. The fire department is sure the fire was set deliberately and someone used a lot of accelerants. I'm saying your ex-wife made that accusation. Obviously we want to talk to your daughter as a matter of urgency.'

'And you're certain her stepfather killed himself?'

'We're trying to follow up on his movements. The fire started at around 1.45am. Certainly his movements warrant investigation.'

'I don't know what to think. Perhaps Marikka's run away. She might be scared? I have no idea what she even looks like now.'

The detective stood up, keen to get rid of the man. He had other things to do - the kidnapping of Mollie Pendleton was more pressing than finding this wayward firestarter right now. He gave his best fake smile.

'I'm sure we'll be speaking again. I hope it will be in happier circumstances.'

'If she's still alive I will find her,' Leon stated as he stood up.

'I hope for your sake you do sir, but a word to the wise. She believes you're dead. Prepare to be disappointed.'

Leon offered a tight smile. 'I know, I know. I have no idea how to face that, but I just want to find her, let her know that there's a home waiting for her.'

The detective nodded. 'Let's hope it turns out like that, eh?'

Leon left the police station in a daze. He'd gone in expecting to identify burned remains and come out with hope she was alive. But where was she? Where would she go and how had she survived? Was it possible she'd set the fire? His little gentle Marikka? Impossible. That had to be her mother, getting one last kick in. She'd always had a thing about her daughter. Please God, let her be found.

NINE

THE GREAT SECRET

Jackson glared at Marikka drumming his fingers on his chair with increasing irritation. This was not what he wanted at all. Furthermore she was another runaway and that meant trouble. And she asked far too many questions. Didn't seem intimidated at all.

Of course with Mika out of action he would still need someone to do everything. It was extremely annoying to be put in this awkward situation.

'I don't get what you're doing here,' Marikka repeated. 'A fish sanctuary in the open sea? Do the fish know?'

'It's too complex to explain to a …'

'To a girl?' Marikka told him narrowing her eyes.

'To a *child*. It's too complex to explain to a child.'

Marikka snorted. 'You must have explained it to Mika.'

Mika looked at her from his bed and grinned, happy to see Jackson getting hot and flustered. Jackson had said little to him actually, especially about where his cash donations came from.

'I'm saving fish for the future,' Jackson began, as if this was all he needed to say.

Marikka pulled a face, quickly interrupting him. 'A fish sanctuary is a great idea for a lake or something, but the open sea?'

'The sanctuary exists,' Jackson insisted. 'Mika will show it to you at the next feed.'

Marikka looked sceptical. 'You feed the fish?'

'Every other day,' Mika piped up. 'And we test the water.'

'So tell me how it works,' Marikka asked again. 'Is it a trick?'

'We're seeding tomorrow's fish with nutrients,' Jackson muttered.

'Great, so you pollute the sea as well as the dunes. Do you have no respect for the environment at all?'

Jackson looked uncomfortable. The girl was way too difficult to keep around. 'Fish are smarter than you think and it's too shallow for trawlers nets. We are trying to provide a safe place for them.'

'I'd like to have a fish's opinion on that.'

'It's true.' Mika insisted. 'He's got a licence to develop a fish habitat.'

Marikka knew it couldn't be legal. It had to be some money making scam though she couldn't see how at the moment.

'You can't stay,' Jackson said suddenly. 'Mika will just have to muddle through.'

'Mika can't work for several days. He has to rest.' Marikka pointed out. 'I'm going to do his tasks. Besides someone has to start cleaning up your mess.'

Jackson was afraid of that and threw up his hands. He didn't want this girl here, but he knew Mika wouldn't be able to do much. He turned to face her. 'Three days. Then you're gone. You understand?' He made his way to the back of the hangar banging things as he went, clearly angry about Marikka staying.

'I'll show you what we do,' Mika said hesitantly.

Marikka stood up and sighed. 'I don't understand why you need all those wrecks if you're running a fish sanctuary?'

'They were already here.'

'Two bad ideas don't make a right.'

Mika smiled. Marikka was going to be more than a match for Jackson, he could see that.

'OK, Mika. Show me what to do. We should call a scrap merchant and have them take away all this stuff. I'm serious. We should clear the dunes.'

Mika shook his head. 'This area's restricted. No one can touch anything.'

'Jackson's here. You're here.'

Mika sighed, deciding to tell the truth at last. 'He works for an environmental group. It's secret. He's got to test the water in case...'

'In case of what?'

Mika shrugged. 'Something happened here, years ago. That's why it's off limits. You aren't supposed to be here. No one is.'

'Rubbish. I've ridden my horse on the beach. No one stopped me.'

'No one from the village comes here. You ask them. They don't even walk their dogs they're so scared of it.'

'Scared of what?'

Mika didn't want to say. Jackson would have to tell her, not him.

Marikka stared at Mika and shook her head. It made no sense at all.

TEN

DANGEROUS CURRENTS

Mika had woken late the next day having gone to bed way after midnight. His legs hurt. He was beginning to suspect that he had an infection. He was all hot and sweaty and that wasn't normal. There was no sign of Marikka. He sat up, his head was throbbing and he was desperately thirsty. He could hear Jackson making tea in the kitchen.

'Marikka?' He yelled, his voice was hoarse. She didn't reply. He didn't know what to do. Maybe she'd gone for a walk.

'Marikka?' He stood up, his legs hurt and it felt like the skin on his thighs was on fire. He looked down and discovered that his jeans were missing. He looked around and something caught his eye hanging from the rafters. His jeans drying. He knew that he hadn't washed them in months. But that meant she'd taken them off him whilst he was asleep. He hadn't even noticed.

'Hey?'

He looked up. Marikka was standing there eating a biscuit.

'Got something for you.'

'What?'

'Two ibuprofen tablets. You're burning up, Mika. Got some bread and milk too. Come on, it'll help with the pain and your fever.'

'You been to the village shop?'

'Someone has to buy some food around here. It's bloody miles away. You guys need a fridge.' She placed some change on the table, which Jackson quickly scooped up, but continued to ignore them both as he ate his oatmeal. She handed Mika a glass of water and two pills.

'Take them. They aren't going to fix your legs, but at least you'll feel a bit better.'

Mika took the pills and swallowed both at once, washing them down quickly.

'I cleaned your wound. We should go back to the vet. I mean it. Don't pull a face. You're sick, Mika. You need antibiotics. I can tell.'

Mika looked up at his jeans. She followed his gaze and grinned.

'They'll be dry soon. You can wear overalls till then. I found some grubby ones in the back that will fit you – ish.'

'You find out anything about the fire?' Mika asked.

Marikka shrugged. 'Headlines are all about that girl that was kidnapped, Mollie someone. Her dad's a millionaire. *The Daily Mail* had a picture of my stepfather though. Said he owed a fortune to the banks. A lot of people left flowers at my house. Everyone thinks I'm dead. I feel guilty, Mika. I should call my friends. They got a picture of me off someone's Facebook page, even I didn't recognise me. Lucky the woman in the shop didn't either. No one even mentioned Deacon. I should tell them I'm still alive.'

'The vet must have told them by now.'

Marikka shook her head. 'I don't think he will. He hated my stepfather.'

She looked away, feeling suddenly sad. She missed the girls, and the gossip, but then again, she wondered how quickly they would turn against her for not calling them and telling them she was alive. She wondered if they all thought she'd burned the house down. She fought against feeling anything. She was determined never to be soppy and emotional. She was alone now and she had to be strong.

Looking around her she couldn't believe the state of the hangar, everything was a mess. There was no sense of order at all and rubbish that should have been thrown out ages ago festered in black plastic bags.

'You never married, did you, Jackson?'

Jackson looked up from his porridge and frowned.

'You make a lot of judgments for a kid in trouble.'

'I'm not in trouble, I'm simply evading it. How can you live like this?' She kicked an oil can across the concrete floor, disturbing a cockroach that hastily scuttled under a bench.

'I know where everything is. As long as no one moves anything.'

Marikka was sceptical, but said nothing.

'And for your information little girl, I was married, once.'

Marikka very much doubted that and she must have shown surprise because he scowled again.

'And no funny looks from you, either. She was like you, always wanting to interfere, always wanting a house and stuff. I kicked her out. If the credit card company liked her so much, let them have her, I say.'

'You must have loved her very deeply,' Marikka said with a smirk.

'Not everyone marries for love,' Jackson said mysteriously.

'I don't think I'll ever marry. Seems too complicated.'

Mika remembered a task he had to do. 'The bathroom pump needs new washers, Jackson. That's why there's no pressure.'

'I said so, didn't I? Has to be some spare washers in the back.'

'You're not fixing anything today,' Marikka told him, annoyed. 'You're ill, Mika.'

'Marry Mika,' Jackson told Marikka with a sly smile, knowing how this would annoy the boy. 'Your toilet will always run perfectly.'

'I'd be scraping dirt and grease off him everyday,' Marikka retorted.

'I'm going to wash,' Mika declared blushing.

'Where? This I have to see. When did either of you ever clean out the tin bath? It's got stuff growing on it, I swear.'

Jackson ignored her and looked up at a wall chart and squinted at it. 'Tide'll be all the way up in ten minutes. Remember you still got to do your duties, Mika. You'll have to go with her, she doesn't know anything about the tides.'

'I know.' Mika grabbed some Pear's soap, a grubby towel and headed for the door. Marikka followed.

Mika glanced back over his shoulder. 'You don't have to watch me wash.'

'I'm not watching. I'm recording it for posterity. Primitive boy discovers bathroom.'

Mika almost smiled as he headed towards the dunes, Marikka in tow.

Marikka was surprised to discover that the sea had travelled miles from wherever it had gone and here it was, not far from the dunes now. Better yet, there was a concrete shower room with just a bit of original tin roof left on top.

'This is where you wash?'

'The pump doesn't work right. It leaks and the water's cold. It's seawater, but it won't kill you. Jackson makes me boil the water for his tin bath. He won't use this cold shower.'

'Let me see, cold shower in sea water or hot water in a filthy bath, I'm overwhelmed.' Marikka sucked in air through her teeth. 'Tough choice, Mika.'

She saw that he'd fitted a new shower head. It had to be freezing out here in winter. 'Is there an actual toilet as well?'

'There's a wooden seat with a hole in it. Told you, I had to dig it out.'

'You get all the best jobs, huh?'

'You're doing the jobs now,' he said grinning, disappearing from view.

'Don't get your stitches wet.' Marikka called out after him.

'I'm only washing my face and hands.'

She heard an electric pump going and was happy that she wouldn't have to pump seawater by hand. She looked up at the ominous grey clouds. Three days and then where would she go? She still had no idea where to move on to. She realised that she was going to miss hot showers – miss quite a lot of things from now on.

Half an hour later Marikka surveyed the scrap metal on the dunes beside the Nissen hangar with despair. The wind blew her hair wildly about her face. What was the point of saving the planet if people like this were intent upon destroying it? She had a terrible feeling of despondency. What was she doing here? How long did she think she could stay free? Maybe she should go back, face whatever trouble would come her way. An image of her mother's angry face swam into view and she shuddered. Why oh why did her mother hate her so? Life totally sucked right now.

Jackson was suddenly at her elbow, swaying slightly in the breeze, his white stick embedded in the sand. She hadn't heard him approach.

'You think this is ugly, but I only see poetry.'

'I don't see what's so poetic about rusting cars.'

'Look more carefully, Miss Stander. Birds' nest in the tallest vehicles, field mice burrowing into the upholstery, all kinds of creatures have made homes in these cars. You see eyesore, I see sanctuary for animals, a place for birds to breed safely.'

'You're just trying to justify the ugliness.'

'Soon this will all be covered by vines and brambles, hardly anyone but the creatures will know it's here. I'm just trying to say that animals don't understand 'ugliness'; they have no aesthetics. It's either good nest or bad nest.'

Marikka didn't want to argue. 'I don't understand how you make any money. Everything is just rotting all around you.'

'We don't own this rubbish. It's been here since the flood. Some of it's valuable. See that old bus? It's a 1937 Southdown Tiger TS7 Greenline Bus. Special tourer with leather seats. You can inspect it if you like. Bound to be some fanatic who'd want to restore it to its former glory. Each one of these vehicles is quite unique in a way, not as disposable as you think. Call it junk if you like – but see that old 1960 Ford?'

Marikka looked but had no idea which car he was looking at.

'Could fetch £10,000 pounds in an auction.'

'Then... why don't you?'

'You think selling this junk would help? Let it rot. Let the birds have it.' He laughed and in that instance Marikka realised that he was totally mad.

Mika signalled to her from the top of the dune and she set off to join him.

'Was he telling you stuff about the cars?' Mika asked when she caught up. She was pleased to see he was wearing the blue overalls with the legs turned up.

Marikka nodded. 'Says they're worth money.'

Mika laughed. 'Might have been once. You know what salt air does to metal? Just rusting junk now, no matter what he wants to believe.'

'What are you doing outside? You're supposed to be lying down.'

'Got to take stuff out to the fish sanctuary and collect water samples.'

Marikka looked at him sceptically.

'This is my job here. I have to show you. Fish food is a special mix.'

Marikka looked at the small dock beyond the dune. She understood it now. The incoming tide had formed a small pool, deep enough to float the boats already. There was a small channel out to the sea between the dunes.

'How far out do we go?'

'A few miles. Don't worry, the inflatable is real tough and the outboard is strong.'

Marikka didn't quite follow how you fed fish in the sea or why they had to collect water samples, but knew she had to earn her keep and make sure Mika stayed safe.

Mika led her to a pile of sacks left beside the boat. They stank.

'What the...?' She protested holding her nose.

'It gets delivered by someone from Brigstock or Alford. It varies.'

'We're throwing this rubbish into the sea? Won't it kill the fish?'

'High-concentrate nutrients. Honest, he's got a licence for this.'

Marikka severely doubted this. It had to be wrong to feed fish anything that stank this toxic.

'I'll come with you, but only because you shouldn't be moving at all. I think I need to take pictures. I'm pretty sure the Environment Agency would be interested in this fish business.'

'Someone came around,' Mika said with a hollow laugh. 'Somehow he made them go away again. Happy, if you know what I mean.' He rubbed his fingers together.

It depressed Marikka even more to hear that people who were

meant to be saving the planet could be bribed. Everything about this place screamed wrong, wrong, wrong.

'Do the fish get a say in any of this?'

'They love it. Honest. There's a feeding frenzy the moment I tip the sacks in.'

'What's down there? Piranha?'

Mika laughed. He limped over to the boat as Marikka heaved the sacks into the inflatable.

'Oh my god, they really stink.' She complained.

Mika started the outboard and waited for her to finish loading the sacks.

'There's lifejackets under the seat. Make sure you tie it on, OK. And sit well away from the sacks.' He pointed to another flat and wide inflatable pontoon pulled up on the sand. 'We use that for the bigger loads.'

'I can't believe I'm helping you poison the planet.'

'Hold on.'

Mika started the engine and pushed off from the dock, wincing with the strain on his bruises. They moved out over the small waves still coming in with the tide.

Marikka wondered what she had let herself in for and if this was a good time to mention she got a sea-sick?

'You trust him?' Marikka asked, once they were well away from the shore.

'He needs me.'

'But do you *trust* him?'

Mika shrugged. He wondered if it was OK to ask for more painkillers yet. His legs and arm were both hurting and his head was throbbing. He knew she was right, he should be lying down, not showing her the ropes.

Marikka hung on to the sides now as they began to hit bigger waves. She didn't feel sick at all, except when she got a whiff of whatever was in the sacks.

'We're heading to a reef.' Mika declared. 'Got all kinds of things down there for the fish to breed in.'

'We don't have reefs. Australia has reefs, we have mud banks.'

Mika shrugged, like he didn't care what she thought. He pointed towards the horizon.

'About four miles out there's a shallow bit. It's all on the charts.'

'Still not a reef though.'

'People used to live and farm out there. The coast was a good five miles further out from here a hundred years ago. It's true.'

'Five miles?' Marikka didn't believe it.

'Not just here. I mean, all the way from the estuary to the point was farmland and villages. The old woman in the post office swears you can hear church bells when the current is right.'

'And mermaids pulling on the ropes,' Marikka suggested; with a slightly mocking smile. 'There is no way five miles of this coast is missing. People would notice.'

'I swear it. There was a huge flood. That's why they put in the flood defences up the coast.'

'You mean those crumbling concrete seawalls in Sutton? That's all that's defending England?'

Mika shrugged. He didn't know why they were crumbling.

Marikka was looking behind her. 'Come to think of it, the canal kind of ends wrong, should be a dock or... Come on Mr. Historian, explain that.'

'Because the last section was washed away in a storm and then the dock silted up. Jackson had to dig a trench so we can get out at high tide, but honest, there was a whole wharf there once. Canal barges came to load up from sailing ships here a hundred years ago. I found some photos, I can show you if you like.

'Why are you testing the sea water? Is it something to do with pollution?'

Mika nodded. 'We have to test fish, the water and sometimes Jackson makes me pick samphire, it's an edible seaweed. You can see it growing on the beach in places when the tide goes out. Boil it and it tastes like salty asparagus.'

Marikka rolled her eyes. 'Seaweed? Sounds delicious. Can't wait.'

'Used to be a delicacy around here. Locals don't eat it now, or the fish. But I do. Sometimes that's all we have to eat.'

'Cow splats are probably a delicacy around here, doesn't mean I'm going to eat any.' Marikka mused. 'The pub serves local fish.' She remembered. 'I saw a sign.'

'Well it probably comes from Grimsby. I never see anyone fishing out here.'

'That's because you're too busy poisoning them.'

Mika pulled a face. He didn't really know how to impress her.

Marikka relented, seeing he was disappointed with her. 'It's OK. My horse used to nibble the samphire too. Had to stop him because it gave him gas. Horses get scared if they fart too loudly. Did you know that?'

Mika laughed and Marikka smiled, relaxing.

'Jackson's not as bad as you think,' Mika said a moment later. 'He took you in after all.'

'He took me in because you can't work. He isn't stupid.'

'Same thing.'

Marikka didn't think so, but she was grateful for a bed, even the primitive one they had offered her.

'You ever had a girlfriend?' She asked quietly. 'I mean, you're not at school and well... this place isn't exactly crawling with girls.'

Mika shrugged. She'd met Jackson, surely she could see no girl would put up with him for long.

Marikka sensed she'd hit a sore point. 'You're very pretty. You'll break lots of hearts, I'm sure.'

'I don't want to break hearts. I ...'

Marikka shrugged. 'Sorry. I was being mean. I haven't had a boyfriend yet. My friends all think I'm retarded or something, but the Brigstock boys, ugh. They must practice being stupid, it's astonishing how...' she paused a moment remembering that she probably wasn't going to see anyone from Brigstock in a very long time now. 'Anyway, Deacon wouldn't have let them near me. He was very possessive.'

'You think a lot about that dog.'

'He didn't even know he was a dog. I swear. He took care of me from the first day I arrived.'

'Must have been strange going to a new home with a new dad and everything.'

'He hated me right off. Tried to make me like him by giving me Monday. But as soon as I'd trained him and got him right and settled, he sold him. You want to know what a breaking heart feels like? Sell your horse and watch your dog die right in front of your eyes.' She knew she sounded so bitter. 'Sorry. I guess I'm still angry.'

Mika leaned back against the gunwale and closed his eyes. His thighs hurt.

'You feeling bad?'

Mika nodded.

'You're red raw around the stitches, y'know.'

'Salt water will help. Fixes everything.'

'This salt water?' Marikka looked out across the muddy waves. 'This grey polluted sea filled with all the garbage you keep dumping into it?'

Mika squinted ahead and corrected his course. He didn't feel like arguing.

'I just need to be still a moment.'

Marikka looked more closely at him and saw he looked feverish again.

'You're really sick. I've got more painkillers.'

Mika shook his head although he desperately wanted them.

'Of course you could just jump into this miracle water and it will cure you...'

Mika tried to smile, but he didn't feel like it. His head was pounding.

Marikka leant over and felt his brow. He definitely had a temperature. Not good. She was looking at the sacks of 'nutrients'.

'Who makes this fish feed stuff anyway?'

'Some man he knows from Brigstock and a farmer in Alford.

'And they make this stinky mess? It has to be illegal, Mika.'

Mika shrugged. He just did as he was told.

'You think too much.'

'That's what my stepfather kept saying. How far do we have to go?'

'Not far now, you'll see a buoy. Ships used to get wrecked there years ago.'

'Is there treasure? Is that why you like coming out here? Is that where the silver broach came from?'

Mika grinned. 'I might show you if you stay long enough.'

'Ay, ay Captain. Be sure to sign up for ten years.'

Mika laughed again. She talked a lot, but he discovered he liked having her company.

Marikka fell silent as they sailed up and down waves that seemed to be getting bigger all the time. The shore had disappeared. They had to be miles out now. She watched Mika check the compass and hoped he knew where they were going.

She finally saw the buoy, taller and bigger than she'd expected, with a flashing light and a mournful bell that sounded as it tipped and rocked in the waves.

'This is the fish sanctuary?' She couldn't hide her disappointment. God knows what she had expected, but it was just the same grey sea rolling underneath.

'You'll see. Loosen the top of the sacks then just tip them over.'

Marikka untied the string, trying not to breathe in as she did so. Whatever was in here was definitely off. She pushed the first sack over and nearly went with it as they rose on a big wave.

'Hold on!' Mika shouted.

Marikka nearly retched as she saw the mixture of oil soaked sawdust and brown pellets slop into the sea. She kicked the next sack out and it fell with a big splash. Then she was over the other side washing her hands, wishing to get rid of the stink.

Suddenly, from out of nowhere, fish appeared. A swarm of thrashing, hungry fish were charging down on the sacks as they sank towards the shallows. The sea was suddenly alive with fish. Cod or mackerel, she couldn't tell but the grey-green colours were brighter than she'd ever seen on any slab in the supermarket.

Mika saw the wonder on her face and she glanced at him as he grinned.

'When did they last eat?'

'Cod eat all the time. Not this rich though.'

'What are they supposed to eat?

Mika shrugged. 'Crabs and starfish, or worms, squid if they can find it. They like our slop best. Jackson won't eat fish.'

The same thought was going through Marikka's head. What exactly were these fish eating? 'I thought the sea was running out of fish.'

'Not around here. But then again, no one fishes in these off these shallows, it's an exclusion zone. I guess the fish feel safe here.'

'I'm not sure fish can tell if one area is safer than another, Mika. I can't believe how many there are. Pretty colours too.'

Marikka wondered if the exclusion zone was anything to do with the bombing practice she'd seen earlier. The fish still churned in the sea around them. It was an impressive sight. Mika let them drift away from the buoy and the feeding fish before he started up the engine again so he wouldn't hurt any.

Marikka worried that it was a dangerous place to break down.

'Do we have flares or whatever we need?'

'No. But we aren't going to break down. I've done this trip a ton of times. Come on.' He looked up at the sky. 'Clouds are thin and wispy, it's going to rain later I think.'

'You're a weatherman too.'

'Don't mock me. You have to read the weather, it's the only way to be safe. Believe me, you wouldn't want to be out here in a storm.'

Marikka said nothing. She knew that. She was actually admiring him and his skills on the water. She began to think that it was a long time since anyone said anything nice to Mika.

'Where would we end up if we kept going?'

'Nowhere, not got enough fuel to get to the other side. Belgium I think.'

'Belgium? Isn't that where the chocolate comes from?'

'Well, you can swim for it if you want.'

Marikka glanced at him but he was teasing.

'I can only do about two laps in a pool before I start crying for help,' she confessed. 'I don't think Belgium is possible right now.'

'Don't think I haven't thought about it,' Mika said suddenly. 'I just wouldn't know what to do if I ever got there, that's all.'

Marikka suddenly understood that Mika was as lost as she was.

'We'll plan an escape, Mika. Soon as you can walk properly again. Must be somewhere we can go.'

Mika shrugged. He had no idea where that place might be.

ELEVEN

FIREBUG

Mr Cole, the vet, had finally read his morning paper with more than a little interest with his lunch. The kidnapping of little Mollie was the main news. Poor child. Worse the police were speculating that the kidnappers might be the same ones who killed their last victim after collecting the ransom. On page two details were emerging about the fire at Brigstock. It confirmed that Marikka's stepfather, Mr Stander was bankrupt and the bank was in the process of trying to repossess his home, not to mention the taxman wanting to seize everything else. Reason enough to burn it, perhaps, but it didn't explain why he had tried to kill Marikka. That was madness or sheer evil. Since he knew the man, he sided with evil.

The police now believed Marikka hadn't perished in the fire, but had no idea where she might be or the whereabouts of her mother and stepbrother. There was all kinds of speculation about what had happened, including a report 'leaked' that Marikka was a firebug and had burned down a shed when she was nine. He didn't know anything about that, but he believed Marikka's account; she was the victim here. The police had given out a number to call if anyone had caught sight of her.

It left Mr Cole with a dilemma. He knew exactly where she was, but would he be doing her a favour by keeping that quiet? Should he contact the police?

He made another cup of tea. He'd think more about Marikka during the afternoon and perhaps pay her a visit in the evening. Yes, that would be the responsible thing to do.

A bell sounded, quickly followed by sharp panicky barking. The first animal of the afternoon had arrived.

TWELVE

A FATHER'S CONCERN

The Rising Sun pub situated beside the canal lock south of Brigstock was quiet this lunchtime. Out front a truck was noisily offloading a new stock of beer and wine. The sky threatened rain. The atmosphere was heavy with expectancy. A barge was moored on the canal and a small lone girl, her black hair tied up with a purple ribbon, was sitting by a card table awaiting customers. There was a poorly written sign set up nearby her table:

Meet Anya - The Girl Who Can Read Objects – Discover if your lover is true or false.

Leon Stillwater was there to meet with Detective Barber, the detective he'd met the day before. The man was off-duty but had agreed to talk to him. He'd made his way to the pub, anxious for any news about his daughter.

They were sitting in the snug. Smokers were gathered outside, so it just left the two of them in there. Detective Barber wasn't saying much yet. He savoured his beer and looked carefully at Leon Stillwater, saw how edgy he was. He had no opinion about the man. Either he was the father and he'd neglected his daughter, or he was telling the truth and the mother was as bad as he said she was and had run off with her. She still hadn't come forward to make a statement.

'I don't get it,' the detective said, at last. 'I mean. I still don't get why she ran away. After all her stepfather was dead. He couldn't hurt her anymore.'

Leon Stillwater sipped his beer and considered his answer. He'd spent a fruitless morning trying to talk to some parents who knew Marikka and even her favourite teacher, a Miss Spottiswood and her nervous German Shepherd called Weed. They were all convinced that

Marikka was dead. They thought him 'odd' for insisting upon looking for her and ignoring the inevitable truth.

They were prejudiced against him, of course. Marikka had always told everyone her real father was dead and they weren't easily persuaded that this ghost of a man could have produced such a beautiful vibrant girl. They never said this, of course, but they all thought it and they weren't at all helpful.

'We're still concerned about Marikka burning down the garden shed when she was almost nine,' Detective Barber said, munching on some salted peanuts.

Leon sighed. 'It's not as sinister as you think. I made a call to a friend who was still talking to my ex-wife at that time. She said the fire was an accident. Marikka had gone to play with sparklers. She loved sparklers and she accidentally set fire to all the fireworks her mother had bought for her birthday party.'

'See it from another side.' The detective said. 'First the shed, then the whole house. Firebugs start young, we know that.'

'Marikka was utterly traumatised by the experience, my friend told me, and my ex, her mother, went completely hysterical and completely overreacted. My friend says she insisted upon child psychologists, then refused to have her in the house and that's why she was fostered. I made a lot of calls last night and finally got the truth.'

'Why didn't she come to you?'

'Because I was in hospital in Europe. By all accounts she ran away to find me, but no one told her where I was. Then they finally told her I was dead to stop her running again.'

'A bit harsh don't you think?'

'You've never met her mother. She is *ruthless*. Marikka was apparently placed in the foster system under a false surname and she never looked for me.'

'Because you were dead. Must have been quite an accident you had.'

'It was a 50 car pile up in Italy during freak snow. I got out of my vehicle and was hit by another car. I had people write to Marikka for me, but all the letters came back unopened, of course.'

'Surely social services must have noticed the name change? When you came back, I mean. You're the father. The court should be able to trace…'

'I found out last night she was fostered in Cornwall. She wasn't in the London system. She was reclaimed by her mother three years later. Can you believe that? Treating Marikka like left-luggage.'

The detective sighed. This wasn't helping find the girl.

'I have looked for her every weekend since I returned to England. I chased down every Marikka on Facebook.'

'Can't be many girls called Marikka.'

'You'd be surprised. She was born with red hair. Her mother chose the name.'

'So you don't think there's any connection with her burning down the shed and the house fire?'

Leon shook his head. 'None. Marikka is one of those kids who was born to take charge. She sees injustice everywhere. Know what she replied when I asked her what she wanted to be when she grew up? She said 'a Judge'.'

The detective smiled. 'A Judge?'

'She was eight at the time.'

The cop nodded, patting his pockets down to look for a cigarette before remembering that he'd quit – again.

'OK, so why did she run?'

'Because she's scared stiff of cops or social workers and all the people who were mean to her when her mother didn't want her anymore. She probably reasoned that with her mother ready to accuse her of burning down the house she'd have no chance to defend herself and be thrown back in the system. I can't blame her for running.'

The detective knocked back his beer and grimaced. 'It's a theory.'

'Everyone I have met up here says her stepfather was a complete bastard.'

'They were going to repossess the house. Could give him motive to burn it. Scorched earth stuff, y'know.'

'You concede that Marikka didn't do it then?'

'Him or her. *Someone* set it deliberately. A crime was committed. She ran, that makes most people I work with suspicious.'

'I told you why she ran.'

'So you did.'

'I'm going to find her'.

The detective glanced at Leon and shrugged. 'There's another theory.'

'What?'

'The dog.'

'The one you claimed shot the stepfather.'

'That one, yes. Mrs Bocanne, who worked as a cleaner at the house, you won't have spoken to her, says Marikka and the dog were inseparable. If the dog attacked her stepfather, it could be because it thought he was attacking her.'

'Trying to shoot her.'

'Possibly.'

'But why?'

'That's why we'd like to speak to her. If you ever find her, you'll have to bring her in for questioning.'

'You want another pint?' Leon asked him, hoping for more information.

The Cop looked at his watch. 'I'm back on duty at five. I guess I can fit another one in.' He signaled to the barman he wanted another. 'Off the record, Mr Stillwater, we're looking for two other men in this arson attack. It might be connected to another case we're working on. I can't discuss it, of course. If your daughter turns up, she still might be guilty. Or she's a possible witness. She may have seen who did this.'

'Another reason she might have run off.'

'Granted. To be honest right now all our efforts are concentrated on little Mollie Pendleton. We're expecting a ransom demand any moment.'

Leon paid for the beers. He got the message. He was on his own. The police weren't going to make much of an effort to find Marikka.

The detective suddenly remembered something. 'Oh yeah, I've got something for you.' He bent down and extracted a blackened and charred book from a plastic bag. 'It won't help much, I suspect, but it's about the only thing we found that proved she ever lived there.'

Leon took it from him. It stank of fire and was damp, but it was unmistakably Marikka's diary. Her name was still visible on the remains of the cover.

'It'll probably fall apart.' He said apologetically.

Leon was grateful to have it. He handled it like it was precious metal.

'Her friends created a Facebook memorial page.' Leon said wistfully. 'I saw some photos of her running at sports day at school. She's tall now. I've missed so much. She calls herself Slim, doesn't seem to use her own name.'

'Which was why you couldn't find her earlier, I suppose.'

'All her friends have left really sad poems and remarks. They definitely all think she's dead.

The detective shook his head. 'I'm convinced she isn't. We'd really like to talk to her. We're issuing a phone number that people can call if they spot her.'

'Turn her in y'mean.'

The cop shrugged. 'We can't turn a blind eye to arson, Mr Stillwater. Can we? If she's innocent, then the sooner we find her and clear that up the better.'

'Go find your kid. Don't really know what I'd do if one of mine went missing.'

'You'd go looking. You'd have no choice.' Leon told him.

He held the charred diary and wondered what he'd find inside if anything.

He stared out of the window at the barge moored besides the canal and the young girl sitting with a female client at a small table. He was thinking about Marikka. If she was alive why hadn't she contacted her friends? Why were they so certain she was dead? What was he missing here?

THIRTEEN

THE GIRL WHO
CAN READ OBJECTS

Anya held the object in her hands and pretended to concentrate, letting her hair fall forward to hide her deep brown eyes. She was aware that Calleigh was watching her. He was always watching her, even knowing she could hardly walk now. He'd made sure of that.

'Make it look difficult,' he'd tell her repeatedly. 'If it looks too easy they won't pay so much.'

She didn't care. First opportunity she ever got she'd leave. Anything was better than being chained to Calleigh the monster, who kept her prisoner, the man who'd stolen her childhood and when she wasn't working kept her chained up below deck, on the barge, out of sight. He told people she was only thirteen, but she knew she was older. She had to be. She had few memories of her mother and they weren't good memories. She still remembered with eternal bitterness the day Calleigh had paid for her in cash. She'd been so little, so defenceless, just eight. She'd had the 'curse' even then, although her mother called it a gift. Been able to do this 'trick', as Calleigh called it, from the moment she could first talk.

She never knew how long the canal was, just that she'd been up and down it for years now. It felt like forever. Always leaving before anyone asked awkward questions, or because he'd picked a fight with someone. He was always arguing with someone. Couldn't help himself.

Now here she was, the 'Girl who could read objects', a fairground freak without a fairground. Friendless. A prisoner prettied-up by her captor, who told her she was getting more attractive every day and she knew what that meant. So far she slept alone, but one day, soon no doubt, he'd be drunk enough to…

They were sitting at her regular table set up beside the barge. A woman was sniggering as she read the leaflet in her hands: *'Discover the truth about objects. Anya is the girl who can reveal the deepest secrets of any object. Find out if your partner is true or false. Anya reveals all.'*

Ridiculous, but it kept the punters coming. She even had regulars. A woman from Thirsk was always giving her objects from her husband's pockets to try and find out if he was having affairs. Right now she had this stupid glittering piece of leather in her hand. Who would put diamonds on such a thing? Must have cost a fortune.

'It's a dog collar,' she told the woman who sat before her.

'I know it's a dog collar. Whose dog collar?' The woman said tetchily.

Anya had no idea why this thing was important to the idiot woman but she thought some more as she handled the dog collar impregnated with little diamonds and silver thread.

'She's very famous. On TV a lot.' (Not that she'd ever seen TV. He'd only allow a radio on the barge and that was always tuned some stupid local radio station that Calleigh liked to call up and loudly abuse until they cut him off).

The woman looked pleased. Anya guessed she'd bought it off e-bay. She'd never used e-bay either, or a computer, but she knew from Calleigh that people bought things on it all the time and came to her to make sure it was genuine.

'It was owned by this woman, blonde, foolish with money. The dog died suddenly. She gave this collar to…' Anya suddenly sensed that there was a real tragedy here. The dog's owner had been really grief stricken. She hadn't given this to anyone. It had been buried with the dog. This was grave robbing!

Anya looked up and moved her hair aside to fix her eyes on the overweight woman with too much make-up and gaudy rings on her fat fingers.

'This collar was stolen from the dog's grave. You shouldn't have this. It will bring very bad luck. Return it. She might be grateful. She missed Pepe very much.'

The woman stared at Anya with surprise, then growing anger.

'I paid two thousand for this on auction. You think I'm going to give it back?'

Anya remained impassive. The woman had already paid. Calleigh made sure of that.

'You sure it was Pepe's collar?'

Anya nodded. It had been a wretched tiny dog that had lived a life of misery, being carried around everywhere in a handbag. She felt sorry for little Pepe.

The woman was laughing, really happy now. 'You're a miracle, girl. That collar is going to be worth twice as much now. Pepe. That was *her* favourite dog. The diamonds have to be real.'

Anya nodded. Of course they were real. The woman had doted on that little dog. She let go of the collar. She didn't want to feel the dog's pain anymore.

The woman grabbed the collar and stood up waving to her friend who was sitting by the water.

'It's genuine, Colin. Can you believe that? She even picked out the bloody dog's name.'

The woman walked off. Didn't say thank you. Anya felt pity for the dead dog and this awful, selfish woman. She fought off an overwhelming urge to scream. Why were there so many greedy people in this world.

Calleigh brought her fresh water and a biscuit. If anyone ever asked, she always had to say that he treated her well. But no one ever asked her directly. No one ever asked why she wasn't in school, or what she wanted, or anything. They were only ever interested in the objects they brought her. It was as if she didn't actually exist.

'Another happy customer,' Calleigh said glancing over. 'She'll tell her friends.' He was pleased the woman was going away smiling. Better than the dumb customers who cried.

'I'm going to the pub. If anyone comes, ring the bell, OK?'

Anya nodded her head. She watched him walk towards the pub. He drank almost everything she earned. It was rare she could keep any money back. Not that a girl who was chained up could spend it. But come that moment she escaped perhaps, she'd have something at least. Enough to get away.

She knew where the key was, of course. He taunted her with that. Inches from the maximum amount of room she could move around in the barge. Kept in a lockbox that only he knew the combination for. She'd touched the box. She knew the numbers. How could he not know that she knew the numbers? She was the girl who could read objects. Now she lived in fear of him threatening to 'marry her' to make it legal. She wished she knew who her father was. Where he was. She was ever in hope that one day he'd be the one who offered up some object and she'd be able to tell him – it is *me* that that you seek. I am your daughter. But, of course, he never came. Worse, he may not even know she existed. She hated even thinking that. In her dreams her father would one day free her from Calleigh. Perhaps murder him, drown him in the canal, punish him for imprisoning her all these years, preventing her from going to school, starving her when he was depressed, beating her when he was drunk...

She'd once asked a teacher for help who'd come to ask her to read an object. He'd done nothing. She'd tried again with a woman, a nun. Surely, she reasoned, a nun would help her, but all she said was that she was a wicked child and must have done something to deserve this fate.

After that she'd asked no one for help. No one cared about gypsy girls who read objects. In the end they just cared about their stupid objects. She was always the girl with the extraordinary gift, but she never saw it as a gift. Gifts were overrated and besides, she did not think it remarkable that every object had a memory. It had always been so for her.

She hadn't registered that a man had sat down in front of her. She had finished her glass of water and was surprised to find him there. She was supposed to ring a bell; particularly if it was a man.

'Are you alright?' He asked, gently. 'Did you want more water? I just bought a bottle. It's fizzy.'

She nodded, but only to regain composure.

'It's twenty pounds,' she told him, hoping it would put him off.

He placed a note on the table and she snatched it up quickly, folded it small and tucked it discreetly into her shoe.

He snapped open the bottle and poured her some sparkling water. She loved sparkling water. Calleigh would never buy it, wouldn't pay for the bubbles. 'Waste of money,' he always said.

'I don't know where to look. I've tried everything,' the man was saying. She sipped the water, appreciating that it was cold.

The man took out a diary. It was blackened and damp, the cover stiff and charred. It had to be recently burned because it still reeked of fire. Had someone not wanted it found? Yet here it was, in the hands of this exhausted man. Was this man her father? She didn't think so. Too white, too tall. Her real father would be dark skinned like herself. She never even knew his name. Just Dadda. How stupid was that?

The man handed over the book to her. She knew from his expression that he was deadly serious and very sad. She would have to tread carefully. There had been a tragedy; that much she could guess from just looking at him.

Anya prised open some of the pages. A photo unexpectedly fell out onto the table. It was of a young girl and her dog. The photo was remarkably intact given the blackened exterior. She was beautiful with wild red hair and looked so happy with her dog, an animal with a proud head. Anya knew instantly that the dog was dead.

'Marikka and her dog. It's the only picture I've got,' he whispered, hardly able to take his eyes of it.

'Say nothing,' she told him sharply.

Marikka was his daughter, but there was a terrible separation between them. There was sadness in her eyes, even though she was smiling in the picture. The diary told of pain, a lot of pain and each page was filled with tears. That much she knew.

'The dog died. Violently.' She touched the photograph and felt

73

the love the dog had for the girl and it was rewarded. The dog was everything to her.

'The dog died for her. She held him in her hands as he died.'

The man looked at her in complete astonishment as tears flowed down Anya's cheeks. The sadness was overwhelming.

Anya looked him straight in the eyes. 'She's alive,' she whispered. She closed her eyes, swaying in her seat. She could feel the girl. She was confused. She was with someone, but she thought she was alone in the world. She definitely did not know that her father was looking for her.

'You're her father? Yes or no?' Anya asked urgently. She normally didn't ask questions, but there was doubt here. Why didn't the girl come to him?

'Yes. She believes I am dead. She was told I died.'

Anya shuddered. Yes exactly. She didn't go to him because he was dead. He even looked like a dead man.

'Where is she?' he asked.

'South of here. South-East.' She pointed along the canal. 'Follow.'

Leon looked down the canal. It was logical, but it ended at the coast – where would she go from there?

'Go to the sea. You will find her.'

The man abruptly stood and knocked the table. It fell on its side and the diary with it. He began to apologise but abruptly stopped when he saw the chain marks around her leg, the red sores on her skin. Their eyes met.

'My god.'

Anya said nothing. She knew better than to ask for help anymore.

'Come with me,' the man said as he righted the table. 'Who has done this to you? I can help you.'

Anya frowned. The offer was genuine, she could tell. She didn't know this man or if she could trust him. She hesitated and then it was too late and immediately regretted it. Calleigh was coming out of the pub; she could sense his movement, even though he hadn't opened the door yet.

'You can't help me,' Anya told the man. 'I cannot leave. He will hunt me down. He has said so.'

The man's eyes widened as she gave him back his diary.

'I will come back for you,' the man told her. He noticed the wiry tattooed man coming out of the pub. 'I will come back.'

Anya shrugged. No one ever had.

'It's twenty pounds,' she said loudly, so Calleigh could hear.

'That's too much I'm afraid. I'm sorry,' Leon replied, understanding her ruse and shaking his head. He walked away without another word.

Calleigh arrived and stared after him resentfully. 'Another bloody cheapskate.' He looked back at the pub. 'Might be a bloke and some bird who wants you to look at something in a moment. I'll make some sandwiches.'

She watched him go across the grass, to the barge. She looked back for the man who'd just been to see her but he had already vanished. She didn't think she'd ever see him again. Calleigh was intimidating. He scared a lot of people. That sick haunted man looking for his daughter would not be back. She closed her eyes, forcing herself to feel nothing, but that dog, that dog in the photograph, it had really loved that girl. She wanted a dog like that, one day. A dog that could bite, keep her safe, attack when she told it to, keep all the men like Calleigh away.

He came back with a plain white bread cheese sandwich for her. She hated his sandwiches; they tasted of nothing and were too dry.

'We're heading back up the canal tonight. Not enough business here.'

Anya said nothing, but her heart sank. She liked it here. People were sometimes nicer. She briefly thought about her last customer. If he'd wanted to help it would be too late. By the time he came back they would be gone and he would shrug his shoulders and lose interest in the gypsy girl. She'd have to save herself – somehow. Calleigh had made sure any escape would be slow. She tried to run one day last summer and he'd let her get half a mile and suddenly there he was screaming at her. Shattered her foot with a hammer and wouldn't let her go to hospital, so it set awkwardly. She could not run now if she tried.

Customers came out of the pub giggling. Shy, unsure, clutching their objects. Calleigh took their money. She watched them approach. She went to work.

FOURTEEN

BONFLEET

The car came for Jackson before light. Mika had watched him go. His mates from Brigstock, the ones who brought the fish food and money and most often brought him back drunk. He hated Jackson when he was drunk, too much like his father. Jackson never told him where they went or what they did, but he didn't like his friends – too many gold rings on their fingers and always in a different car. Most likely stolen. He tried to sleep a bit longer but his legs throbbed too much and wouldn't let him. He knew he should let doctors see his wounds – he was being foolish. Knew that.

He woke Marikka at hour later, at dawn, although she didn't look so happy about it.

'It's still dark,' she groaned.

'It's almost light. Jackson's gone and the tide's all the way out.'

'So? I could have slept in. You know how hard it is to sleep in here. It stinks of boys and diesel.'

'We're going to see the lost town.'

Marikka blinked. 'The one with the ghost bells?'

'I can't promise bells, but the tide is going to be at its lowest for months. Best time to see it.'

Marikka began to dress. She looked at him carefully. 'You OK today?'

Mika shrugged. 'The stitches still hurt like hell and I feel weird, but maybe better than yesterday.'

Marikka nodded. She made sure to bring the painkillers just in case, he didn't look much better at all.

'Roll up your jeans and forget your shoes, it'll be wet,' he said. 'You'll thank me later. It's where I found the silver broach.'

'Isn't it cold? I'm freezing.'

'I thought you were tough.'

'I'm a tough girl who likes being warm. And where will I dry my only set of underwear if I get wet? Oh genius of the deep?'

'You know where the washing line is. Besides I have spares.'

'Clean spares?'

Mika hesitated for one fatal second.

'Ugh. Thought so. You're such a boy.'

'Come on, stop arguing. Let's go.'

'Don't get your stitches wet, remember?'

'It's salt-water.'

'Oh yes, I forgot. Miracle cure for everything.

Marikka reluctantly followed him outside. It really was freezing. The sun was barely on the horizon, but at least there wasn't any wind. She was thinking that given that Jackson had gone somewhere they could have slept in a while.

Mika walked ahead on the cold, cold sand. Marikka couldn't believe it. The sea had completely vanished again. It was miles of sand ahead.

'Who stole the sea?'

'I told you,' Mika shouted back. 'It goes out for miles this time of year. Especially under a new moon.'

Marikka ran barefoot, splashing through pools filled with stranded starfish, jumping over mudbanks, and slowly she came to understand just how beautiful it all was. The dunes were already tiny in the distance behind her. She had the feeling they were the only people in the whole world. Mika was walking slowly way behind and she ran back to him feeling guilty because she could see he was in pain.

'I'm sorry. I got excited.'

Mika smiled. 'Don't be. I love this place in the mornings.' He pointed to some small white birds wading in the rock pools, hunting out worms or shellfish. 'They love it too.'

'Do you know their names?'

'Wagtails.'

She took Mika's good arm, concerned that he was doing this for her but should be back in bed. 'You sure you're OK, Mika? We could go back y'know?'

Mika shook his head. 'I swear he did the stitches too tight, that's all.' He was annoyed with himself. He hated being sick.

'How big was this place anyway?'

'I don't know. Bonfleet was built on a small mount. I guess they thought they were safe from the sea.'

'This was all fields at one time?' Marikka was looking over the whole sweep of the beach and trying to imagine it as grassland with cattle on it or whatever they had. It was impossible.

The sun was finally rising above the horizon and caught the tip of a long buried building, some metal on the roof glinted momentarily dazzling them both. Marikka stared opened-mouthed. There really had been a village buried here.

Mika pointed out the remains of stone walls and rusted railings.

'A bus.' Marikka exclaimed. She stared at the rusted remains of a single decker bus.

'Jackson said that was driven out here ten years ago and got stuck. It's not ancient or anything. You can only see this when the tide gets this low. Watch where you put your feet, there's jellyfish around here and they can sting.'

Marikka could see the translucent creatures, slimy raw eggs lying like unexploded bombs on the surface and skirted around them. Something shiny and blue caught her eye half buried in the sand. She knelt down and began digging around it to reveal a long blue metal sign. 'Players' it said in a fancy white enamel script, but she didn't know what it meant. Perhaps a sports hall, or something.

'Jackson says that most of this coast will disappear one day,' Mika said.

'Most?'

'Y'know. Climate change.'

Marikka did know. Her stepfather had emphatically declared that climate change didn't exist except to raise taxes from everyone.

Yet right here there had been a whole village with a church and everything, all buried, all gone.

Mika was sitting, scrabbling away at the wet sand, peeling a huge orange starfish off a rock and carefully brushing sand away from around it. He pulled something out from between two shells and tossed it towards Marikka. 'Here.'

She picked it up. It was shiny on one side with encrusted green stuff on the other. A half-crown with a King on one side. She could just make out the words George V and 1923 in the circle. She wondered if it was valuable. It was in good condition considering where it was. 'I've never seen one of these before.'

'Lots of coins here, and other stuff. Look.' He rolled over and pulled out a small dark green bottle, the stopper missing. 'Scent bottle maybe?'

Marikka was suddenly happy they had come out here. All these lost treasures from a forgotten place. A crab darted between his feet and another was trying to bury itself in the sand.

'Don't people come here and dig it up?'

Mika shook his head. 'It's off limits to the public. Didn't you see the signs? No one is supposed to come here. Besides it's too dangerous. Soon as the tide turns you have to run for it. People have drowned further down the coast.'

Marikka looked up at the sea, still some distance from them.

'Don't worry, we're safe.' He told her with a little smile.

'We are?'

'I think.'

'You think? Then what, a huge tidal wave comes in and ...'

Mika grinned. 'That would be so cool.' He held a large starfish up for her to see. 'But seriously, the tide does come in super fast.'

Marikka wished she had a camera. Here she was on the beach of a ghost town. It felt very special.

'Thanks, Starfish Boy.' She smiled at him.

'For what?'

'Bringing me here.'

He grinned, content to see her look happy. He had nothing to give her but this, his secret place. They climbed a slippery wall and there before them lay a church spire tumbled from grace, lying prostrate on a mud bank, the rusted cross sticking out over a large shallow pool. He placed the starfish into the pool.

Mika pointed towards more crabs running across the remains of the wall. Marikka went forward to look more closely and when she got to the other side she knew for sure the church bell would never sound again. Half a huge bright green copper bell was buried in the sand with hundreds of tiny starfish lining the inside whilst baby crabs were crawling in the wet sand.

Mika joined her. 'Jackson wanted to dig it out. Said the bell would fetch a fortune, it's copper. But I wouldn't let him. Some things should stay where they are.'

Marikka looked at the coin in her hands and wondered if it was right to take it. After all it had been a long time since anyone could spend half a crown.

'You think anyone drowned?'

'Lots. Jackson said there were five hundred people living here one time. No one in the village will talk about it. It's like they have am-knee-whatsit.'

'Amnesia?'

'Yeah, that. No one I ever met from around the village remembers anything about Bonfleet. All the rusting cars on the dunes you hate? Jackson says they belonged to the people from here. He says it was a conspiracy. The Government let them drown. Don't get him talking about it – he's obsessed with this place. Says terrible things happened to the people and it was all kept secret.'

Marikka had a bad feeling now and suddenly threw the coin into the bell cavity. 'I don't think I should keep it.'

Mika was surprised, but understood.

'Five hundred people? Here?' Marikka queried. 'There's not even a street or anything. You sure?'

Mika pointed further out towards a mudbank and the remains of another building.

'Street was there somewhere and there was a wall and a harbour. I bet if you dug you'd find houses and shops and remains of the fishing boats. Bits get churned up in a storm and still wash up on shore.'

Marikka stared, but she couldn't picture it or how a whole village could have so completely vanished.

'Jackson says that the whole sea out here was once grassland and swamps ten thousand years ago. Doggerland he calls it.'

Marikka shrugged – she wasn't convinced anything Jackson said was true.

Mika looked back at the waves for a second and sensed the tide would soon turn. 'Come on, we have to get back.'

Marikka took Mika's hand. 'Take it easy. We have to make sure your stitches don't tear anymore than they already have.'

Mika was surprised that she was holding his hand and discovered he liked it. 'You won't tell anyone about this place?' He asked quietly.

She shook her head. 'It's your secret, Starfish Boy. It's safe.'

Mika smiled and they walked slowly back towards the shore. It looked far, far away. Marikka felt relaxed for the first time since her house burned down. Mika was a wild boy and needed civilising, but his heart was right. He needed to be rescued as much as herself. No way was she going to leave him behind with Jackson.

The sun flared across the sand exposing ridges and shallows. Starfish lay stranded everywhere and other shellfish, all waiting for the tide to return. Some air bubbles appeared revealing shellfish were buried in the damp sand. Marikka discovered that the whole beach was alive.

'I need breakfast, Starfish Boy.' She said suddenly. 'I can't believe how hungry I am.'

Mika felt hungry too, but his legs were hurting with every step. He looked down and saw the blood had soaked through the bandage on his left thigh. He wondered if he should go back the vet. He didn't say anything to Marikka. She was looking happy and it felt good that he was the one who'd made that happen.

'It's really beautiful here,' she said, enjoying the warm morning sun on her back. She pointed at the hordes of wagtails feeding in the pools of water. 'A place like this should definitely be kept secret.'

She turned to call Deacon and her face momentarily fell. Deacon wouldn't be coming.

FIFTEEN

THE GOVERNMENT MEN

Marikka stared at the rows of seemingly inconsequential rubbish that lay on the racks at the side of the hangar. As she stared at the bits of plastic or household items, baskets, bottles and broken chairs she realised that each one was tagged with a name and date. She recognised that this was stuff that washed up on the beach all the time but why was it tagged? How weird was that? Here she was thinking Jackson odd but perhaps there was method to his madness. She examined an ordinary cane shopping basket labelled January 2010. 'Safe'.

Safe from what? She wondered.

The front door suddenly slammed shut, a gust of wind blew through the hangar and with it the scent of afternoon rain. Jackson was back.

He was removing his jacket when he saw her down by the racks. She could see he looked exhausted – a man with a hangover - she could smell the booze on him from where she stood and wrinkled her nose. All his actions were stiff and awkward.

'What are you doing?'

Marikka shrugged. 'Wondering why you collect all this stuff. I mean, there's empty washing up liquid bottles and even odd baby socks.'

Jackson turned away, snapped the cap on a bottle of water, popped two pills into his mouth and took a swig from the bottle.

'You don't know what this place is, do you?' He said after a moment.

Marikka wondered if that was a trick question. 'It's a former bomber hangar. Mika said they used to fly from here to bomb Germany.'

Jackson sat down on the tattered leather chair – another rescued item from the dump no doubt – and removed his muddy shoes. Marikka could see he was shaking from the effects of the booze. His hands trembled slightly and she wondered how old he was. Forty? Fifty? She had no idea of how to tell a person's age.

'Second World War was a long time ago,' he told her. 'You going to make a cup of tea or just stare at me?'

Marikka moved towards the kettle and took water from his bottle to fill it. She looked at the dirty cups and made a mental note to bleach them, god knew what bugs lurked in this old place.

'This base was still active all the way up to 1985,' Jackson told her. 'No one could get near it or the beach until about ten years ago. That's when I moved in here.'

Marikka's eyebrows shot up. 'You've been living like this for ten whole years?'

Jackson shrugged. Ten years was a long time in anyone's life.

'Was that when Bonfleet drowned?' Marikka asked, as she washed the cups out. She noticed he had holes in his socks. Jackson was falling apart like all the things on the racks.

Jackson narrowed his eyes. 'What do you know about Bonfleet?'

'Only what I can see at low tide.'

A cloud of anger passed over Jackson's face. 'Did that boy take you there? Where the hell is he anyway?'

'He's sick. He's got a temperature. He should be in hospital.' She didn't want Mika to get into trouble, so she added, 'anyway, I went for a walk this morning and I found the ruins. Had to be Bonfleet.'

'Don't go there again.' Jackson said sharply, bearing his yellow teeth. 'Never go near it. It's dangerous.'

'It's just old bricks and walls. How can it be dangerous? It's underwater most of the time anyway.'

Jackson closed his eyes in annoyance. 'Until you know the facts, you can't have any opinion about Bonfleet. Get that? You don't know what happened.'

The kettle boiled, she poured hot water on the tea bags. 'Well tell

85

me then. I'm not a kid. If there's something I should know, tell me. I want to know why you test the water all the time. Is anyone paying you to do it? Are you hiding out?'

She handed the hot mug to Jackson and he took it and cradled it between his hands. Marikka noticed his nails were almost white and the tips of his fingers burned. She wondered how long it took to recover from a fire and how it happened?

'Didn't you worry about the cars on the dunes, Marikka? Didn't you notice they're all old, nearly forty years old in most cases. Shouldn't you ask yourself why they're here?'

'I… I know it's a disgrace they're on the dunes. This is supposed to be a nature reserve. You tell me the birds and animals like it, but I don't buy it. They need a natural environment, not rusting cars.'

Jackson glared at her. 'What they are, is a monument to folly. That's what they are.'

Marikka puzzled over that statement for a moment. Not sure rusting cars could be a monument to anything except waste.

'They teach you about climate change at school?' Jackson asked.

'Yeah, of course.'

'Well let me tell you that Bonfleet stood proud for hundreds of years out on the spit. Storms came and went, but it survived. Good sea defences and the way people thought there was that it didn't matter if the sea did go around them, at least they'd be cut off from interference. Some people wanted it to be an island. Five hundred people made their living there. Fishing mostly, but there was a cannery and farming where the beach is now. There was the church and they were a religious god-fearing lot, a lot of people who live by the sea are. A close community, didn't mix with the inlanders much, except to fetch in a bride or two every so often. Bonfleet was a special place right the way up until 1970.'

Marikka sipped her tea discovering that the milk was on the turn. She'd have to buy more tomorrow.

'It was an experiment.' Jackson added.

'What kind of experiment?' Marikka was thinking about the

weather maybe, something to do with climate change. She was beginning to wonder now why she hadn't learned anything about the place.

'Might have been protection from fall-out from the atomic bomb. The world was still thinking that there would be a World War Three with nuclear bombs back then. That was one story. Or it might have been a cure for the common cold. No one knows, no one is admitting anything. It was very secret. Bonfleet was selected exactly because it stuck out from the mainland. It was remote with five hundred secretive people who kept to themselves. They didn't even have TV, couldn't get the signal back then. The Government knew that if they came here, no one would ask awkward questions. They offered money to make people agree to it, but I don't think they knew what it was they were getting into.'

Marikka began to sense that this was Jackson's story. This was why he was here. He was from Bonfleet. Had to be.

'The government scientists came and administered their poison to everyone and then left.'

'You saw this?' Marikka asked.

'I *know* this. I was a youngster then, working on my Dad's fishing boat. Just the two of us and we'd be gone two weeks at a time. Dad and me sailed into Bonfleet harbour, small but with high walls against the sea, and we discovered there wasn't a soul left alive. Not a soul. Dogs and cats were running around hungry but everyone was dead. Mothers and children lay in their beds, their faces wracked with pain. Some people had gone and shot themselves, the pain was so great. We found sixty-five people in the church who died on their knees praying. My own mother died in the bath, covered in sores. My younger sister, Arlene I found dead in the garden, her left arm swollen to twice its size. She left me a note telling what happened. Even left me an envelope with the money they'd given her to take part. Fifty quid. That's what each and every life was worth to them in Bonfleet. Fifty bloody quid.'

Marikka shut her eyes. She could see them all in her head lying dead in the church. Jackson looked down at his tea, inhaling the steam.

'We couldn't even bury them. Couldn't touch them. Didn't know what had happened or what they had given them. Helicopters were coming and we knew that we had to get out of there quick. Dad wanted to shoot the chopper down but I got him onto the boat and we sailed out of the harbour pretty fast, our catch still in the hold.'

Marikka said nothing. She shivered. It was truly horrific. Jackson must have been traumatised; he'd been so young.

'We watched what happened from a mile off shore. Dad had his binoculars. I couldn't look. They waited till low tide and then dumped all the bodies in the harbour. Then they brought bulldozers in and demolished the houses and tipped all the brick and stone into the harbour on top of them.'

'And no one saw?'

'No one. It was a military area you see. You had to drive through it to get to Bonfleet. They worked all through the night. They knew this secret could never get out, so they did something the sea had never managed to do; they blew up the sea defences. I saw that with my own eyes. Blew it up right and left to make sure the sea would overwhelm the town. They had luck on their side. It was a full moon and high tide. Dad knew from the way the pressure was dropping that a storm was coming and we had to put in at Scarness.'

'Which means?'

'Without the walls, the sea would swamp Bonfleet. They did their job too well. Didn't realise that the wall was protecting a huge stretch of coast behind it. The storm came in and battered Bonfleet into submission – swept all the cars and bus and pretty much everything people owned to here.'

'And it was just left like this?'

'Old military base. Restricted area. They didn't care about the environment back then. Just as long as Bonfleet disappeared, that was all they wanted.'

'But it must have been on the news. You couldn't possibly hide a town disappearing.'

'Oh, it was on the news all right. Four hundred and ninety-eight people 'drowning', he put up his index fingers to punctuate it. 'Claimed they drowned in their beds from a sudden freak wave that destroyed the sea wall and demolished the town. Pictures on the TV the next day horrified people. Everyone was calling for better sea defences. Some people wondered why there weren't any bodies. Government claimed they'd all been swept out to sea and no one was allowed in to look (as it wasn't 'safe', they claimed).

It took just two months for pretty much everything to disappear under mud and sand. The fields were swamped and in two years it became a beach. Now you, or anyone who walks here thinks it has been this way forever.'

'And no one knew you and your Dad survived?'

'Dad knew that if we revealed what we had seen, or that we were alive, they'd probably shoot us. If they could make that many people disappear like that with no questions asked, they could easily kill us. Dad died of a broken heart a month later and I wanted to follow him. We were living with a family we knew in Scarness and took up their name. Me Dad was the type of man who'd sooner cut his own throat than tell a lie but ...' He swallowed hard remembering something. 'The Jacksons looked after me well.'

'You never got over it. Is that why you're here?'

Jackson shook his head.

'I went to work in a market garden in Boston. Couldn't get Bonfleet out of my head though and when I began to hear about people dying of strange illnesses around here I came back. I get help from an environmental group in Sweden and I test the water and anything that comes out of it in case.'

'The fish sanctuary is a cover.' Marikka realised.

Jackson nodded. 'Everyone is long dead but that's why Mika and me gather the samples. We test everything that comes from Bonfleet. Fish, shellfish in particular. People around here eat the fish and shellfish and the mortality rate is higher around here than anywhere else in England. I swear there's a link.'

Marikka took a deep breath. 'But you can't do this forever. You aren't well yourself. And why won't you let Mika go to hospital? Surely no one is looking for you now? You don't even have the same name.'

'They never forget. The environmental agency comes every once in a while. They just think I'm squatting here and leave me alone as it keeps other squatters out. They could make me leave if they wanted to. If Mika goes to hospital, they'll ask questions about me. He's a runaway, like you Marikka. Once social services get involved...'

Marikka nodded, she understood, but Mika still needed help.

'How did you get burned?' Marikka asked suddenly.

Jackson drank some of his tea. 'Milk's going off.'

'I know. I'll get more tomorrow. If you had a fridge it might help. How did you get burned? Was it an accident?'

Jackson shook his head. 'I got drunk. I get depressed if I get drunk. I don't really remember much, but they found me in Scarness, in my car. If I was paranoid, I'd say someone set fire to my car. But I was a smoker then. If you drink whiskey and smoke...'

Marikka winced, she didn't want that image in her head at all.

'And don't go talking to anyone about Bonfleet. No one will believe you and you will lead people to me. Understood?'

'But if you ever find evidence of whatever they used to kill everyone.'

'Then I'll have a Swedish Environmental Group to protect me. Until then I watch and wait and one day I'll join everyone else at Bonfleet and it will be forgotten.'

Marikka thought it very sad. Jackson was wasting his life here for something he couldn't ever fix.

'I have to check on Mika. He needs something to bring his fever down.'

'He'll live.' Jackson said, sipping his tea and staring at the wall.

Marikka wasn't so sure.

Mika was half awake, his lips chapped and he was burning up. She made him sit up and swallow two more pills and the rest of the water.

'I'm going to take you back to Mr Cole tomorrow,' she told him as he sank back onto the pillow.

He nodded. He wasn't going to protest. He knew he was proper sick now. Should have gone to hospital.

'He been telling you about Bonfleet?' He croaked.

Marikka nodded.

'You believe him?' Mika asked.

Marikka frowned. 'I think so. Sounds horrific. Funny how no one ever talks about it though. I mean, I've ridden Monday on this beach, seen people walk their dogs here. You'd think there'd be huge warning signs to keep away – aside from the bomb practice.'

'I wonder how they kept it secret?' Mika whispered. He closed his eyes and went back to sleep.

Marikka wondered about that too. Could a government get away with killing so many people? Even back in 1970? She'd seen Bonfleet with her own eyes, but was it really big enough for five hundred people? It was a lot to think about.

Jackson loomed over her as he made his way to his bed. 'One day I'll make those bastards pay for what they did,' he muttered. 'One day I'll be able to prove it.'

Marikka watched him go. She discovered she wasn't afraid of him anymore.

SIXTEEN

SAVING ANYA

Anya was below deck, chained up as usual. It was late, Calleigh was drunk. She could hear him on deck sloppily filling the tank with fresh water. Once he'd got the tanks filled they'd be on their way. She'd had a wash and was preparing for bed. She wondered where they were going. He liked the cities, but some people in the cities didn't like the girl who read objects. Some called it witchcraft and were darkly superstitious. Sometimes she feared that they would attack the barge. Calleigh didn't stop in these places even though he knew there might be some good customers.

She suddenly heard footsteps on deck. Then shouting. Something sharp fell against the side, metal clanging. Perhaps someone had come to rob Calleigh. There were always townsfolk who thought there was hidden money on the barge. It had happened before when he was drunk and talked too much at the pub.

She heard Calleigh shout, but now the tone of his voice was of a man in pain. Then silence. She waited, sensing someone moving about on deck. She heard a thump as something heavy fell to the deck. Her heart beating wildly, she tried to concentrate, to conjure up a vision, but she couldn't and she was shaking with fear. Would she be next?

Suddenly the hatch slid back. A face peered down into the darkness and shone a torch on her.

'You all right?'

It was *him*. The ghost man who'd seen her leg. The one who was looking for his daughter.

'I'm chained,' Anya said quietly. She felt a surge of hope, but tried to suppress it. Where was Calleigh?

'Is there a key?'

The man climbed down. He found the light switch on the wall, always an inch out of her reach. She saw his head and arm were bleeding.

'You're cut.'

'He pulled a knife.'

'Where is he? What happened? Is Calleigh…?'

'Don't worry. He can't touch you now.'

The man was looking around the cramped cabin, seeing her bunk, saw how little length she had on the chain and could feel the anger flowing through him as he understood what conditions she lived in.

'Key?'

She pointed at the lockbox on the wall, always out of her reach. '9019.'

He punched in the numbers to the lockbox and fished out a key. He quickly came back to her. She raised her nightgown to reveal the heavy metal clamp around her leg. She wasn't afraid.

'My god, this is medieval.'

He unlocked it and the clamp fell to the floor with a loud thump.

'Get dressed. Do you have anything you want to keep?'

Anya shook her head 'Why are you doing this?' She knew why but wanted to hear him say it.

'You will help me find my daughter, then I absolutely promise we shall find you a home, a safe place. Do you have a name?'

'Anya.'

'Is that your real name?'

She had no idea. There was a dim recollection of another name, but it was all gone now.

The man was taking deep breaths, trying to calm himself after his fight with Calleigh. He was clutching at the blood oozing from his arm.

'First-aid in toilet.' Anya pointed out, discovering she was still shaking.

He nodded and quickly entered the tiny toilet, scanning the shelves for a red cross box, spotting it behind some shampoo bottles.

'Get dressed, Anya. I want us out of here in five minutes,' he told her.

She quickly pulled on her clothes. She found her thin red coat, with worn sleeves. Something Calleigh had stolen from a car. This was all she had.

He was already on deck waiting for her, wrapping a bandage around his bloodied arm. She came up, nervous in case Calleigh counter attacked, but there was no sign of him.

'Calleigh?' She asked, biting her lip with nerves.

'I told you he won't bother you anymore. Come on. We've got to move.'

She joined him on the canal bank and he took her hand leading her away from the barge. She had no idea of what had happened to Calleigh. Couldn't believe he'd give her up so easy and all his drinking money.

Leon glanced back. He was sure no one would come this late. In the morning people might come looking. But not now.

'He won't come after us?' She asked, nervously looking around into the darkness with alarm. She could sense he was close but yet far away.

'He'll never find you again. I can promise you that. You're limping?'

'He broke my foot.' She told him plainly.

He swore, gripping her hand a little tighter as if it could instantly fix things for her.

They stopped by a motorcycle. 'Put this on.' He handed her a helmet to wear. It was his own and far too big for her, but she put it on anyway and strapped it as tight as she could. 'I'll get you one that fits tomorrow.' He added.

Anya felt weak at the knees. She was getting away. It was really true. She was getting away. She looked at the man in the glare of the streetlight as he winced putting a plaster on his head cut. She had to trust him. She'd promised herself that she'd never trust anyone as long as she lived, but she had no choice, she had to trust this man. Who was he?

'I have faith in you,' he told her as he got on first. 'Climb on.'

Anya climbed on the back wondering where to put her feet.

'First we will find Marikka.' He told her showing her where to put her legs.

Anya closed her eyes as she felt the pulsing motorcycle underneath her. It was new. She smiled and slipped her arms around him, appreciating his warmth. She liked new things. They had no memories at all.

SEVENTEEN

SEA-MYTHS

Mika slept fitfully that night and twice Marikka got up to wipe his forehead and make sure he was all right. Jackson snored on, of course. Nothing was going to wake him.

First light found Marikka awake and agitated. Something about Jackson's story bugged her. She wished she could Google it. There had to be something on Wikipedia at least. That many people couldn't just disappear in England and no one make a fuss.

That's why she was back on the wet sands, enduring the bracing breeze, retracing her steps back to Bonfleet. Her hair whipped across her face. It was freezing cold despite the early morning sunshine. The tide was once again miles out from the shore. Crabs and all manner of shellfish were crawling in the shallow pools as she strode out barefoot on the rippled sand. She had to skirt a deep pool and a sandbank where thousands of jellyfish had been stranded. She had a terrible loathing of jellyfish having been stung when swimming in Spain when she was eight. Couldn't even look at them they creeped her out so much.

Bonfleet was further out than she remembered. She eventually reached the half-buried church bell, the abandoned rusted bus and the seaweed covered walls on the mound. But if the whole village had been buried; why not these remnants? Explain that Jackson. She wanted to see more. The tide was still on the retreat, well on its way to Holland it seemed, so she felt safe to go further. If five hundred people or more *had* lived out here she was certain there would have to be more evidence that they existed, some ruins, at least a trace of a buried harbour.

Seagulls struggled against the breeze, their strangled cries comforting somehow as they sailed by almost in slow motion. She paused when she heard a familiar whinny on the wind and turned to see someone galloping their horse on the wide firm sands closer to the shore. She felt a twinge of jealousy. Sensed the confidence of the rider, saw the steady daisy cutting action of a happy horse on firm sand. So long now since she'd ridden herself. Did Monday still remember her? She hoped so. She'd never once gone to see him, hadn't dared, knew it would break her heart.

She looked back at the cresting waves rolling down on the sand. She was in a direct line to the church ruin. There was nothing here. Not a brick. Not a stone. The sand and mud had covered everything. Was that actually possible? Bonfleet was like Atlantis, buried so deep now it was totally forgotten. It might as well never have existed.

She glanced back at the shore. Could the sea do that? Completely eradicate a human settlement? Leave no trace? Why had the church ruins survived and nothing beyond it? Surely there had to be something? Why would Jackson even make it up? Made no sense to her at all.

She started the long walk back. She was more full of doubts than ever. If there had been five hundred people here there would have had to be a schoolhouse, shops, roads. Why wasn't the church buried along with the rest of it? Mika might believe this story but everything in her head told her that this was just a fantasy. But then, why was Jackson hiding? What was he doing? Feeding fish? What was he really up to?

As she walked she thought again of Monday and how ecstatic he'd been pounding on the sands. She realised that she didn't want the dead of Bonfleet to be real, because this beach was the one place where she had been full of hope and happiness. Deacon had gone crazy here, running in and out of the dunes, barking at seagulls, sleeping beside her in the tent, growling at anything that went by in the garden. They had all enjoyed their week in the wild at Mr Cole's and she didn't want that memory destroyed.

On reaching the dunes she looked back at the distant waves once again. She'd decided. Nothing Jackson said was true. He was a liar.

She had to get Mika out of there as soon as he could move. That boy definitely wasn't safe.

She was still working out how to persuade Mika to leave when Jackson asked her to get milk and food from the village store. It would be another long bike ride. He looked more shifty than usual. All her instincts told her that something was up, that he wanted her well out of the way, which meant he was expecting visitors. He was constantly checking the time, keen for her to get going.

Mika was still sleeping, sweating up. She reluctantly left him alone and headed out down the track to the road. Part of her was glad to escape, but leaving Mika so ill back there? She should call an ambulance. Do the right thing by him. That's what she should do. She knew she wouldn't call though. He'd only hate her if she did.

At the top of Blackness Lane she paused by the phone box. Call the police? Hand herself in? Call an ambulance for Mika? Do one or the other at least. She steeled herself to make a decision and swung open the door. The phone box had been vandalised – there wasn't even a phone attached to the severed wires. She guessed no one needed phone boxes anymore - except to wee in – judging from the foul stench.

She let the door swing back and put it down to fate. It didn't want her to make any calls.

It began to drizzle as the wind grew stronger. She'd probably get soaked going back - typical.

She finally made it to the village store, parked the bike outside – hoping it wouldn't get nicked – not that this old boneshaker with the bent saddle was very tempting for anyone.

The white haired woman behind the counter was distracted by her crossword and ignored Marikka as she gathered her shopping. She was searching for the potatoes when she noticed a ginger cat curled up on a sack of 'Lincolnshire's Finest Spuds'. He opened one eye to discourage her from disturbing him. Luckily there was a plastic bag of 'whites' with a reduced price sticker on it she could take instead.

'Don't let that cat intimidate you.' The woman called out, noticing

Marikka's confusion. 'The tatties in the sack are fresh dug – you'll find them better tasting than those. Micky, let the girl into the spuds now. Just move him dear. He's always lazing around. Supposed to be chasing mice.'

Marikka gently reached under the cat and took out four large 'reds' and the cat didn't budge one bit. Just opened one eye as if to challenge her to move him. She laughed as she withdrew her hands.

'He knows what he likes.'

The woman snorted. 'Thinks he owns this place he does.'

Marikka brought her shopping to the counter. The woman looked like a local to her, probably lived here all her life.

'Were you living here in 1970?' She asked. 'Y'know, when Bonfleet drowned.'

The woman looked at her with a puzzled expression. 'Bonfleet?'

'Y'know. Out there, on the beach. Used to be a place called Bonfleet. Five hundred people drowned when a big wave came in and …'

The woman pulled at a loose strand of her hair and stared at Marikka as if she were mad.

'Never heard that one before. Whoever told you that?'

Marikka blushed. 'Someone who used to live there. I saw the ruins. There was a church and …'

'Ay, I grant you that. There was a church and a village. I've been out there walking myself, but in 1970? I was a teenager then my girl and them ruins were pretty much as they are now dear. Five hundred people drowned? I think the *Lincolnshire Echo* would have mentioned it? Don't you? Even back then the tele news would have been down here looking for bodies.'

'So you don't remember a flooding?'

'Last flood was in the fifties dear, well before I was born.' She pointed to the front of the shop. 'Take a look for yourself. On the wall, over there by the noticeboard.'

Marikka moved back towards the door and found a community news board with announcements of a Whist Drive in Mablethorpe and a charity walk to Scarness. Beside it was an old black and white framed photo of the shop as it was in the fifties during the flood. A man wearing huge waders was in a boat helping a young woman climb out of the top floor window. She realised that the whole shop had been under water.

'Water rose all the way to the ceiling in the bedroom upstairs. That's me Mam being helped out of the bedroom. Married that bloke she did. My Dad, Henry. Bless him. Died ten years ago now. Loved this village he did.'

'So this area *was* flooded.'

'Ay, a February tide it was. Right bad too, took years for trees to grow again after all that salt in the ground. I don't rightly know how many died – a few hundred I suppose, right along coast all the way down to Lowestoft. But never five hundred in one town. It was worse from them in Holland of course. My Dad was a fisherman and he told me nearly two thousand died over there in Zeeland. The sea rose over 18 foot overnight. Imagine that. They had it terrible. But never that many folk from around here. Someone's been filling your head with nonsense, I think.'

'But the cars on the dunes. Weren't they washed up by the flood tide?'

She made a face. 'No, dear. That was the military. They closed the base, put everyone out of a job here and left all their rubbish behind. Years now we've been telling them to tidy it up. Get nothing but empty promises. We're the village that time forgot, that's us. Bloody eyesore. It's a wonder anyone comes here for a holiday at all.'

Marikka suddenly saw the rack of newspapers beside the door. The headline read:

£250,000 MOLLIE RANSOM– Police demand 'Proof of Life' from kidnappers.

Below that story she discovered a photo of herself - it had to be at least two years old when she'd worn her hair up and she was on Cleethorpes boating lake with Rachel.

'MISSING TEEN WANTED FOR QUESTIONING BY POLICE'.

Marikka nervously went back to the counter and quickly offered the woman money for the groceries.

'People are all full of nonsense.' The shopkeeper was saying as she rang it up.

'You staying down here for a holiday?'

Marikka nodded. 'Just a week. Half-term is early this year.'

'Teachers always on holiday or strike – how kids get any education beats me.'

She gave Marikka her change and went back to her crossword.

Marikka made a swift exit, making way for a large woman entering with a shopping bag. She gave Marikka a quick penetrating up and down stare that quite freaked her out. She remembered that they didn't like strangers around here.

She'd only just loaded up the bike and set off down the road when she heard the shop doorbell clang again. Instinctively she looked back. The two woman were shouting something at her. One was clutching the newspaper, the other speaking on her mobile to someone. Marikka didn't need to hear what they said, she knew she'd been rumbled.

Head down she kept riding, going the opposite way to what she wanted to throw them off. If they'd called the police it would be ages before they turned up. If they ever turned up. Everyone knew that. She kept riding, confident that once she reached the caravan park she could duck down behind it to the dyke and ride to the beach along the pathway there.

The flashing blue lights of the approaching police car surprised her. How on earth? The cops NEVER responded. Not out here. She swore and swiftly turned onto a bungalow driveway letting the bike fall as she ducked down behind an old Fiat in the hopes that the cops hadn't seen her.

Out of the corner of her eyes she saw a net curtain flicker. Nervous old eyes were fastened upon her as the cop car whizzed past on its way to the shop. Marikka didn't waste any time. She picked up the bike turned it around and got off the property before they too called the cops on her. She was a one-girl crimewave around here.

Heart in mouth she pedalled through the caravan site at speed, hoping no one was watching. She rolled the bike down to the dyke and pushed it under the road bridge. They'd be looking for a girl on a bicycle not on foot. It was annoying, as now she'd have to walk. She looked along the path quickly realising that she'd be exposed to the road once she got half way along. Sneaking back up the grassy bank she could see the blue lights flashing in the distance outside the shop. The bloody women were no doubt all agog to tell of their brush with the evil firestarter.

She'd been away from Mika for hours now. She was scared for him. Jackson would let him die rather than call an ambulance, she knew he would.

Traffic rumbled over the bridge overhead as Marikka hesitated. She bit her lip, had no idea which way to go. She was hungry. She tore off the end of the loaf. Let Jackson complain if he wanted to - not her fault he lived so far from the shop and now it was bloody raining and the bike was rubbish. She needed food.

She was about to set off again when she heard a motorcycle stop above her. More cops? She couldn't believe it. She hunched down. Prayed they wouldn't have the gumption to look for her under the road.

Leon stopped his motorcycle on the bridge, noting the cop car with flashing lights that had just overtaken them had stopped at the village shop. He turned to Anya.

'What did you say? I couldn't hear you.'

'She's here, Leon. I swear it. She's here somewhere.'

'You sure?'

Anya could feel her skin on her head prickle. Marikka had been here, she could sense it. Recently too. If only she could touch something she had in her hands. The old burned diary was no use to her. The fire had consumed her presence.

Leon was looking at the police car ahead. Probably another break in. The countryside was practically lawless, there were so few cops to cover it. He did think of asking them if they had news of Marikka, but then again he didn't want to explain himself all over again. The cop in Brigstock said he'd call if he heard anything.

'What do you want to do, Anya?'

Anya was confused. Marikka had been here – recently. She was positive. It was if she could reach out and touch her. 'She's close, Leon. We have to stay near here. She's hiding near here. I know it.'

Leon sighed looking around him. But where was she? In the caravan site they had just passed? Hiding in a barn somewhere?

'I'll park up. We'll knock on some doors. All right?'

Anya nodded. They were so close. It was maddening.

Mr Cole was feeding his dog when he heard gentle tapping on the kitchen window. He opened the back door to find Marikka standing there looking soaked to the skin, pensive and embarrassed. She was still wearing the same clothes as before and her hair was bedraggled. She looked desperate.

'Someone in the shop called the cops on me. My picture is on the…'

She saw the *Lincolnshire Echo* on his table. She didn't have to say anymore. Mr Cole saw what she was looking at and nodded.

'I know. Come on in. Maybe it's time for you to talk to the police, Marikka. You can't run forever. You have to face this thing y'know.'

'Mika's ill, Mr Cole. High temperature, feverish. The skin around the stitches is red raw. I'm so worried.'

Mr Cole was already flustered from a distressed dog someone had brought in earlier. He sighed opening the door wider. Marikka could see one of his hands was bleeding.

'Why haven't you called an ambulance for him? I told you that there was a risk of infection.'

'No phone. He won't hear of it.'

'Who won't hear of it? The boy?'

'Jackson. He's the one living in the hangar. We're at the old air base about half an hour's walk from here.'

Mr Cole frowned. 'You're living there? Surely it's uninhabitable'

The dog growled beside his dish seeing Marikka as competition for his food.

'Don't mind Nuisance. He hates to share his dinner. Kettle just boiled. Make yourself some tea. There's muesli if you want to eat something. I just need to treat my hand. Got a nasty bite from my last customer.' He paused examining his bloodied fingers on his left hand. 'And then we'll talk Marikka. Please don't disappear this time.'

Marikka nodded her head and closed the door behind her.

'I'm sorry about before. I was scared.'

Mr Cole waved a hand in dismissal. He understood.

'Don't make a mess. I'll be back in a moment.'

Marikka took a deep breath and made some tea. She helped herself to two bowls of muesli. All her life she had taken for granted the fact that food would always be in the kitchen at home. Muesli was already an impossible luxury now.

She was nursing her mug of tea when he returned, a fresh bandage wound around two fingers. She noticed the patches on his jacket sleeves and wondered if Mr Cole was making any money stuck out here far away from a town. Most likely not.

He poured himself a cup of tea and sat down across the kitchen table.

'I can help your friend for now. But he should be in a hospital, Marikka. He needs x-rays. I only stitched up what I could see. Who knows what other damage there might be. I can call an ambulance and it would be there in half an hour. This Jackson character has no right to deny that boy his life. You understand? If an infection has got in, he could risk septicaemia. Do you want that on your conscience?'

Marikka shook her head.

'What is his objection to the boy getting help? Is it religious?'

Marikka didn't know where to begin.

'Just tell me what's happening, Marikka. Your running away isn't

104

helping any either. I know you must be scared. There was an item on the radio about you this morning. The police are asking for your mother to come forward – she's disappeared with your little brother and they're looking for you as well.'

Marikka stared at her tea feeling guilty and sorry for her step brother. Not that they'd got on much. Her mother doted on him. He had nothing to worry about. Little brat knew it too and was always keen to get her into trouble any chance he got.

'My mother will tell them I started the fire. She hates me, Mr Cole. I promise you on a stack if bibles I had nothing to do with the fire. It was my stepfather.'

'I have no worries about you telling the truth, Marikka. I've had enough to do with your stepfather and your mother to know your situation. I'll give you something to take to the boy, but I want you to come back here. Understand? You can stay with me. You can help me with the animals. Heaven knows I need help these days. There's not enough money to pay for help in this practice.'

Marikka looked up and saw he was being genuine.

'But the boy?'

'He belongs in hospital. He needs help. What is he doing living with that man anyway? Is he a relative? Is he 'safe'? What do you know about this strange man? He's squatting there isn't he?'

'Mika's a runaway. He knows if he goes to hospital that they'll send him back to his father. He's deathly scared of his father. He was beaten, Mr Cole. He's a drunk.'

Mr Cole frowned. 'Then I'll make sure social services get to him first. He needs to be in a proper caring foster environment. He needs to be going to school. Not driving and crashing cars on our dunes.'

Marikka knew Mr Cole was right. Mika probably wouldn't see it that way, but living with Jackson was wrong.

'Jackson's a fugitive too,' she confessed after a moment's thought.

Mr Cole narrowed his eyes. 'Tell me more.'

'He's been hiding from the Government for years. He says that the Government experimented on the people of Bonfleet. They killed nearly five hundred people and then destroyed the sea walls so it would drown. He was a boy then, but he's been hiding ever since. That's why he's testing the water and got this fish sanctuary out in the sea. But I'm not convinced, Mr Cole. I think *he* might believe it, but the woman at the village shop doesn't remember anything about it. I'm beginning to think it's just something he made up to shut me up.'

'The Government killed five hundred people? Here? And no one noticed? Fish sanctuary in the North Sea?' Mr Cole asked, his voice raised with incredulity.

Marikka shrugged. 'He's got Mika convinced. He's testing the fish and water and anything that washes up for poison. He says he's looking for evidence to prove that they deliberately destroyed the town.'

Mr Cole blinked. 'When did he say this happened?'

'1970. That's why he won't have an ambulance there. That's why he doesn't want Mika to go to hospital because it'll all lead back to him and then they'll …'

'It has to be nonsense.' Mr Cole's declared. 'I've lived around here most of my life, apart from when I was serving in the Army. I never heard of this. Five hundred people don't just disappear without trace in this small community. Hell I doubt there's more than two thousand people living here altogether. If that many died people would talk about it forever.'

Marikka shrugged. 'It's what he told me. It sounded real. They buried the people under the old harbour and then demolished the town and dumped the rubble over the bodies. They were a very secretive community.'

'In 1970?'

'Yes.'

'Have you seen the ruins yourself?'

'Mika took me out there at low tide. I saw the old church steeple lying on its side and there was a rusted bus and some old stone walls. But I looked again this morning and...' her voice trailed away.

'You couldn't see anything. The tides will do that. Shifting sands and all... But if five hundred people had lived there, that's a lot of homes, Marikka. There was a Church. That's a fact. Dated back to Saxon times I heard, but...'

Marikka nodded, glancing up at him as she clutched her empty mug. 'It's just a story isn't it.'

Mr Cole stood up, his brow furrowed. 'I'll be back in a jiffy.'

He left the kitchen a moment. Nuisance his dog trotted after him. Marikka decided to fill the kettle. She needed more tea. She wondered if he had a spare toothbrush. She was desperate to brush her teeth. All these little things she couldn't do anymore. She suddenly remembered that Mr Cole had said she could stay with him. Help him with the animals. She realised that she'd love to do that. In memory of Deacon. That would be a good way to pay him back for being so loyal.

Mr Cole returned, as promised, with a large rolled up sheet of paper in his hands.

'Bought this at a car boot sale last year. Thought it might come in handy one day.' He spread it out on the table, placing his mug at one end to hold it down.

'Ordnance Survey map of this coast. It's dated 1965. You seen one before?'

'We looked at one in class once. Studying hills and rivers and how towns were formed.'

'Good. Then you'll know this is a map that shows not just where a town is, but the heights of hills and the whole topographical information you need to get around. Useful for hill climbers.'

Marikka waited to find out why he was showing her this old map.

'The thing of it is that not much changes really. Not inland anyway. A hill's a hill, a river might break its banks from time to time, but generally goes back to the line of least resistance and that's already been established over eons of time.

'Now take a look. Show me Bonfleet.'

Marikka leaned over, following the coastline from the north of the map to the south. She frowned. Bonfleet wasn't there. She looked up at Mr Cole

'I can't find it. He said something about a spit.'

He pointed to a swirl and some tiny writing.

'There might have been a spit at one time. Bit like Spurn Head on the Humber which is also slowly disappearing. But if there was ever a spit off this part of the coast, it hasn't existed for a hundred years. Look, here's your church marked. St Olaf, no less. Norwegian - 1020 AD. Over a thousand years old. See the cross. He was the King of Norway for a time until defeated by King Canute.

'You mean there really was a King Canute? The one who tried to ...'

'Turn back the tides at Bosham, allegedly. A long way from here, near Chichester.'

'So there was a Viking settlement here.'

'Yes. Quite likely. Bonfleet was probably built around the old St Olaf church. Fleet means flowing water and you've seen how fast the tides are. My guess there was an older Norse name for the settlement and somehow it got changed to Bonfleet, meaning good flowing water - possibly. Like nearby Saltfleet, which used to be much more important than it looks now.

Marikka could make out the words *1927 Floodline* near where Bonfleet should be and pointed to it.

'1927?'

'Bonfleet was abandoned after a terrible storm in 1927. It continued to exist of course, but the sea is powerful and it slowly disintegrated. I imagine people used to come and forage for souvenirs and the like, but then the whole area was made into a military zone in 1938 and no one was allowed on the coast there for years. There was another devastating flood in 1953 and I imagine the rest of Bonfleet was destroyed at that time. The old military base has been a disgrace for a long time, all those abandoned vehicles. Absolute eyesore.'

Marikka thought of Mika living with a crazy man.

'So what Jackson told me is...?'

'A story to stop you calling an ambulance, I suppose. You need to get that boy out of there, Marikka. Who knows what that man is up to? Or what he's hiding.'

Mr Cole looked at the clock.

'I'm going to get you something to give the boy. Two now, then one every six hours. If his condition doesn't improve in twenty-four hours Marikka, you'll have no choice. Do you understand me? It won't be about making him feel better, it will be about saving his life. Are we clear about that? I'm breaking a lot of rules here – so don't let me down.'

'Yes.' She sighed. If it wasn't for Mika she wouldn't go back there at all.

'And my offer is still open. Get the boy right, or into hospital, and then come here. We will tackle your mother and all comers together. You're not alone, understand?'

Marikka took his good hand briefly and squeezed it. 'Thank you.'

'Meanwhile, go grab a shower. I left a towel out for you. The pills will be ready for you in ten minutes. You want me to drive you back?'

'No. I don't want to spook Jackson.'

Mr Cole smiled. 'You're a good person, Marikka, but sometimes people will take advantage of that. Now go, get yourself clean and don't...'

'Make a mess...' Marikka trilled, smiling for the first time in ages.

EIGHTEEN

SEEING GHOSTS

Leon emerged from the toilet to rejoin Anya. They were sitting in a run down pub on the Huddlebank Caravan site road having the 'special' – baked potato and tuna. It was filling at least. They'd had no luck so far, but Anya was convinced they were in the right area.

The server, a woman with tattoos on her fat arms and straggly peroxide hair came by to bring the ketchup that Anya had asked for.

'Is that your bike out there?' She asked, looking out onto the car park.

Leon nodded.

'My son rides one now. Terrifies me. I'm always fretting he'll have an accident.'

'It's not the bike riders,' Leon told her. 'It's the motorists you have to worry about. As long as he's wearing his leathers and a helmet he'll be fine.'

She made a face, not convinced. She looked down at the photograph of Marikka and Deacon lying on the table. They'd already asked her if they'd seen her. 'If I were you, I'd go see the vet, Mr Cole. He's a good dog man. He gets all the gossip. If anyone has seen her, he'll know. Go down the private road by the old windmill. Last house by the dunes.'

Leon smiled. 'Thanks. I'll make sure we do.' He didn't think he would though. Marikka's dog was dead, she had no need to see a vet.

Anya was thinking as she ate. Leon smiled at her. He felt guilty making her look for Marikka, knew he'd have to make it up to her, whatever it took.

'Slow down Anya, you'll choke.'

Anya smiled wiping her mouth. 'Sorry. I'm so hungry. Hot food. I never got to eat much hot food.'

'Don't think I'll feel sorry for you, Anya. Living the life of luxury on a barge all your life. No school. No homework.'

Anya frowned, was about to take offence, then noticed he was grinning and trying to make light of her life on the barge.

'I've got so much to catch up on I think.'

'How did you learn to read?'

'Taught myself. Someone once told me that it was impossible to teach yourself, but I did. Calleigh bought me a spelling book and I used to practice my words at night. I made myself memorise twenty words a day for years.'

Leon was impressed. Anya was bright and surprisingly tough. He guessed she had to be to survive.

'We should go see that vet,' Anya said, her expression serious.

'Why?'

She shrugged. Anya couldn't explain it exactly. 'We just have to go there. She loves animals right?'

Leon nodded. He couldn't see the point, but this was Anya's show now. He had to respect that.

'She's hiding here somewhere. I know it. No one has seen her, but people will talk to the vet. The woman was right. We should have gone to the shop too. Y'know, where the police were.'

Leon thought about it. 'You're right. We should have spoken to the police. My error. I apologise.'

'You think she's been here before?'

Leon smiled. 'Well, she loves the beach. I took her to Calpe in Spain once and she dug a hole in the sand and said she wanted to live there. She was about seven. Sulked for hours when we finally dug her out.' He grinned at the memory.

Anya noticed Leon sounded more like a normal person now. She liked his name, it sounded like lion and she wanted someone strong to keep her safe. She still worried Calleigh would get free somehow and come after her.

'Do you think she'll want to see you?' Anya asked. 'You being dead all this time?'

Leon stared out across the car park to his motor bike. It was the one major worry he had. That Marikka would reject him. She wasn't to know how many long hours he'd spent looking for her, trying to track his ex-wife down. There had been no trace at all, nothing. She'd closed bank accounts, taken everything and been really thorough to make sure he'd never find them.

'I hope so, Anya. It's all I can hope.'

Anya wondered if her own father had ever looked for her and what she'd say to him if he ever appeared. She wondered again if he even knew she existed?

'What do you do?' Anya asked him as she ate her potato.

'I'm an illustrator.'

Anya wasn't sure she understood what that was and kept her silence. She didn't want to appear stupid. Leon could see she didn't understand.

'Drawings for books, advertising, anything really. I work freelance. Gives me time to look for Marikka.'

Anya had an image of him working in her head, drawing. Working on a computer. She understood now.

'What about you? What do you want to do?'

Anya looked surprised for a second. No one had ever asked her that before.

'I don't know - never had a choice before.'

Leon looked at this serious girl opposite him and knew that he had to make good on his promise to find a safe place for her. He had friends, they would help. This was one child, at least, who would not have to suffer anymore.

NINETEEN

EARLY WARNING

Jackson was angry and trying to pull himself together as he searched for his passport. He hated being put under pressure, always one last favour to be made. He should never have agreed to the fish sanctuary in the first place, never mind the rest of it. Too late now. The money had been too good to turn down. With Mika wounded and sick he knew it was a sign. Time to move on. He'd known the moment the girl arrived that things would change, something about her attracted trouble. He opened another old tin and finally found his passport. The picture didn't look much like him anymore. He wondered if that would cause problems. No time to worry about that now.

The boys from Brigstock were outside. They seemed edgy, as if they didn't trust him anymore. He knew only too well what happened to people they didn't trust. He had no choice in the matter. They always paid in cash and he was definitely ready to get out of this miserable hellhole.

'Mika?'

He didn't get a reply. Remembered the boy was sick. He wondered when the girl would come back. If she would. More fool her if she did. The boys from Brigstock wouldn't like that. Wouldn't like that at all.

Jackson went outside to join his visitors. He slammed the door behind him hoping it would wake up Mika. Didn't matter much now if he slept or not. Soon he and the girl would be gone. No traces. Take-the-money-and-run-Jackson, that's who he was. Shame about the boy though, idiot for getting himself banged up like that.

But Marikka was already back. It was almost high tide by the time she'd walked back from the vets. She'd approached the dunes cautiously, half expecting the police to turn up at any moment. She'd been surprised to find that Jackson's visitors were still here. They had a crackling driftwood bonfire burning out front of the hangar and their heat-flushed faces could be easily seen in the light of the flames.

She'd had to go to the bathroom when she arrived and it was only when she emerged keeping to the dark shadows that she realised who the men were. It was a shock of recognition. She shook for a moment wanting to run. It only confirmed everything bad she thought about Jackson. She now knew she *had* to get Mika out of there – tonight.

She found Mika at the back by the dock gathering rope and materials together.

'Hey.'

Mika turned. He looked really sick. He seemed surprised to see her. 'You're back.'

'Had to go fetch food and then they called the cops on me. Had to wait until it was dark to get back. You OK? You don't look OK.'

Mika shrugged. He was angry with her for leaving. Jackson hadn't said anything about her going for food.

'Those men back there with Jackson. I recognise one of them.'

Mika doubted it. He just shrugged.

'They're driving an Audi now, but I swear they were driving a Landrover the night my house burned down. They were with my stepfather. I swear it.'

'They come here all the time.'

'They said they'd deal with me later,' Marikka said, biting her lip.

'Might not be them. Did they see you just now?'

'No, but Jackson may have told them who I was.'

Mika looked at her with concern in his eyes. 'If he has they haven't done anything about it. Take a walk or something. Stay out of sight till they're gone.'

'I don't want to leave you here. Come with me.'

Mika shook his head. 'You don't know it's them. Could be a coincidence.'

'How do you think Jackson really makes his money? It's got nothing to do with Bonfleet, Mika. He lied to us. He's getting money for doing something here, but no way is it to do with saving the bloody fish.'

Mika sighed. He was feeling bad and irritable.

'Not everyone is a crook.'

'Jackson is. I swear it. I swear those guys are trouble.'

Mika shook his head. 'Nothing happens here. Those guys appear about once every two months. They're investors in the fish sanctuary.'

'How do you invest in a fish sanctuary in the middle of the North Sea? It's stupid.'

'Because one day that reef will be rich in cod and Jackson will be a hero.'

'Cod?'

'Or mackerel.'

'But no one will be able to fish it, Mika. It's a sanctuary. The fish will be off - limits. If they can't fish, it's worthless.'

'All you think about is money.' Mika still had a horrible throbbing headache. He didn't need all this. She was imagining those guys were after her. Who could be bothered with a runaway kid. No one, that's who.

'You can't get rich off something you can't sell and Jackson isn't exactly a saint.' Marikka pointed out.

'You're wrong. He's doing good now. This sanctuary is a good thing.' Mika snapped. The worst thing was that he knew she was probably right. Jackson always claimed the sanctuary was 'for the environment' but he never did anything unless it had a price on it.

Marikka offered him two of Mr Cole's pills.

'I went back to the vet for you. He's given me these. You *have* to take them, Mika. OK? Now. I've got more. If they don't fix you I have to get you to a hospital.'

Mika glared at her. 'Not going to any hospital. I told you.'

'Then take the poxy pills.' She snapped.

Mika snatched the pills from her hands and put them in his mouth.

'You'll need water.'

Mika shook his head and swallowed them.

Marikka was impressed. She couldn't ever swallow pills easily. 'Nice party trick. Now tell me why you aren't in bed?'

''Cause we're going out to the sanctuary.'

'Now? At night? Us?'

'Yeah. At night. Had you been here you could have help me get stuff ready.'

'I told you. I had to get food and then I had to hide from the cops.'

Marikka was beginning to regret not having stayed at Mr Cole's. The more she thought about helping him with the animals the more she liked the idea. She glanced to the front of the hangar. Maybe Mika was right, she ought to hide until those guys had gone. At least they had beers to occupy them for the moment. Maybe Jackson hadn't told them who she was yet, or maybe he had and they were biding their time. She didn't know what to do.

Although it was true she hadn't got a good look at the men from Brigstock on the night of the fire, she'd seen at least one of them with her stepfather quite a few times. Her mother had warned her off asking questions, but she instinctively knew that they were crooks. She remembered she'd asked her stepfather why he liked them. 'They can make anyone disappear,' he'd answered, as if he'd meant to impress her. 'Even you, Maggot. And no one would ever find you.'

She'd shut up tight. He only ever called her Maggot when her mother wasn't around. She didn't want to give him any excuse to make her disappear.

Marikka stealthily crept to the corner of the hangar and stared again at the men around the fire – cracking jokes – seemingly relaxed. She was finally sure. These were her stepfather's friends. The point was, why where they here? What possible business had they got with Jackson, of all people?

She rejoined Mika at the dock.

'I definitely recognised one of Jackson's visitors.'

Mika put his finger to his mouth. 'Your voice carries at night.'

She winced. The wind had dropped and it was quiet down by the water here. 'What's with this raft?'

'It's a pontoon. We're taking it out to the reef.'

'No. It's too risky at night.' She definitely didn't want to go out to sea at night. Not on this.

'Jackson's towing us out there. We have to take it out there whilst it's fresh.'

Marikka looked out across the sea. It was calm now, but it was pitch black out there with only the stars to see by.

'Is it safe? I mean at night? Anyway you shouldn't be going anywhere, Mika. You're still sick. Look at you, you can hardly stand straight.'

'You scared of the dark? Come on. I'm taking the pills. '

'I'm scared we'll get lost.'

'I've got a compass.'

'You've got an answer for everything, genius.'

Marikka was looking back at the hangar and the cigarette smoke hovering over the men. 'I know it's them. One of them is a Romanian called Olly.'

Mika looked surprised and Marikka knew that she'd scored a hit.

'What the hell are we taking out to the so called reef anyway?' Marikka asked.

'Fish nutrients. High concentrate, like before.'

'And this won't wait till morning? We did this yesterday.'

'Special order. It'll stink even more then. Jackson wants it gone now. Get some water, OK? There's some bottles in the cooler in the boat. And grab biscuits. Looks like we aren't going to get any supper.'

Marikka suddenly remembered the half-eaten loaf and the milk. She'd forgotten it. Left it outside Mr Cole's house. Stupid. She felt guilty.

Marikka scrambled over to the boat and raided the cooler. She found water, biscuits and a flashlight. She quickly brought it all back to the pontoon and stashed it all in a side locker.

Mika was dragging a rudimentary wire cage off the dock onto the pontoon. Marikka understood instantly why it couldn't go on the boat; it was way too big. She gave him a hand and they dragged it to the centre for better balance.

'The sack hangs from a hook in the middle and we lower it off the back.' Mika explained. 'The fish eat right through the sack.'

'You're kidding? How long does it take for the fish to eat through a sack?

'A few hours. There's thousands of them living down there.'

'Why would they just sit there waiting for you to turn up with some scraps?'

'There's always fish. I've dropped lots of these cages down there. Seaweed grows on it and fish feel safe to breed. That's the habitat thing Jackson devised.'

Marikka wasn't impressed, thinking that there had to be a lot of rusty metal on the seabed where once the fish could roam free without bumping into anything.

Mika grabbed one of the water bottles and drank almost half of it in one go. The pills were making him thirsty.

'You want some?'

Marikka took the bottle and swigged some of the water.

'I still don't get this. I swear I learned something about fish and I don't recall them hanging around in one place to eat. They have to roam, follow the nutrients.'

'Even if there's no fish, they'll come. They can smell this stuff from miles away. Really.'

Marikka wasn't sure she believed him, but it was his sanctuary, he had to know what he was doing.

'Those guys haven't left yet. It's cold.'

Mika nodded. 'I brought sweaters. Yours is the black one.'

Marikka found them and pulled the black one on. It stank of diesel but at least it was warm. Mika pulled his on and went to work on the air pump to top up the pontoon.

'How long does this thing stay inflated?' Marikka asked.

'I'm just topping up, that's all. About 24 hours.' He looked back at her. 'Don't worry. I've been out there lots of times in this and it's never leaked yet.'

Marikka didn't say anything. 'Seems funny to do this at night. No lights, no one knows you're out there.'

'We do most things at night around here.'

'Which means whatever he's doing is illegal.'

'He's got a licence. Don't say nothing about day or night.'

'Licence? For real? I bet he just downloaded something off the internet.'

Marikka heard a motor starting. Jackson's visitors were leaving. She wondered what scheme they were cooking up and if they had recognised her. Jackson must have told them who she was. She wondered if they'd be back for her later.

Jackson was standing outside the hangar, beside the Audi, listening to the big man with the bull neck.

'She's big trouble,' he said. 'The last thing you need is Marikka Stander being here. Make sure you get rid of her Jackson. Her stepfather was always saying she was like an albatross around his neck. She's trouble and she'll call the cops on you. He swore that it was her that brought him all that bad luck with the tax bastards. She was spying on him for them.'

'Is it true her dog shot him?' Jackson asked, curious.

'That dog got what was coming to it. Get rid of her. The boy too. He knows too much.'

'I feel bad about the boy.'

'One day they're going to inspect that reef of yours, Jackson. How long do you think you'll survive after that? Quit whilst you're ahead.'

'Is that what you're doing?' He asked them.

'We're going to Spain first flight tomorrow morning. This was the last job. Time you disappeared as well.'

Jackson had been afraid of this.

Olly handed Jackson a fat envelope. 'No need to count it. We're square. Client paid extra. He wants this one gone tonight. Guaranteed.'

Jackson nodded and pocketed the money. He could feel the notes, had glimpsed the stack of fifties. He knew they wouldn't cheat him.

He knew too much about them.

'It'll be done.'

'It better be. Disappear yourself, Jackson.'

They left, spinning wheels in the sand. The heavy sack lay on the sand beside him. He thought he saw it twitch. He kicked it and it remained still.

'Mika?' He shouted, then remembered the girl would have to come for it.

'Marikka? I know you're here. Come here now, and bring the wheelbarrow. We've got work to do.'

Marikka heard the men leave. Her first instinct was to run. She could be at Mr Cole's place in thirty minutes. He had a phone. He could call the police, but on second thoughts, they were still searching for her. The last people she needed down here was the police. Her mother would have done a good job on her by now. Probably be wanted posters on every lamppost:

'FIND MARIKKA STANDER BEFORE SHE BURNS YOUR HOUSE DOWN. CALL BRIGSTOCK POLICE NOW.'

'Coming,' she shouted as she searched for the wheelbarrow.

'Over by the thorn tree. Better hurry up, he gets irritable.' Mika pointed.

She grabbed the wheelbarrow and made her way towards the hangar. She really didn't think it was a good idea to go out on the sea at this time of night.

The sack was heavy and she swore she could smell bleach. If this was for fish, then why give them bleach? Made no sense at all. She hefted the sack into the wheelbarrow, struggling to get it in there it was so heavy, aware she was getting blood on her hands. The sack had to be to be at least her own weight or more.

'Fish food,' Jackson muttered.

'Any reason the sack stinks of bleach?'

'I can't smell bleach. We don't feed bleach to fish. You're mistaken.'

Marikka didn't reply. It took all her strength to keep the wheelbarrow going straight. She knew she wasn't mistaken about the bleach. She pushed the wheelbarrow over towards the dock and Mika attached a hook to it and hauled it up into the wire cage using a small block and tackle.

'Heavier than last time,' he said. 'Stinks of ...'

'Bleach,' Marikka said. 'What's in there? There's blood.'

'Animal stuff, offal. Fish love it.'

'Sharks will love it. Jeez it stinks bad.'

Mika looked at her with a small shrug and smile. Marikka made a face. She was already off fish from the last lot of stinky stuff they'd chucked into the sea. She bent over the edge of the dock to wash the blood off her hands. Hated this, absolutely hated it.

'You guys ready?' Jackson called from the boat. He'd got the outboard engine started and was taking up the slack on the pontoon tow ropes.

Mika signaled thumbs up.

'I think Jackson would like me in that sack, feeding the little fishes,' Marikka muttered as she climbed onto the pontoon. 'He gives me the creeps.'

Mika said nothing. He held the cage steady as the tow rope tightened and the pontoon began to slide away from the dock.

'Did you check the weather, Mika?' Jackson queried.

'A cold front developing, some fog later. Calm sea.'

That seemed to satisfy Jackson. He was checking his watch. The moon was half way up the sky now and bright, with streaks of clouds forming on the horizon.

'Don't worry. We'll be back by one at the latest.' Jackson told them.

Mika suddenly swore. 'I meant to take a leak before we left.'

'World's biggest toilet out there,' Marikka replied. She was glad she'd gone earlier. She didn't fancy hanging off the edge of this rubber mattress and trying not to fall in.

'What do we do?'

Mika lay down on the rubber and shrugged. 'Nothing yet. When we get there we push it off.'

'But it's heavy.'

'Soon as we get it near the edge it'll tip over. The trick is not to go with it. Done that too.'

Marikka laughed nervously. She could so see herself going overboard and being nibbled to death by hungry fish.

'Did I mention I hate cold water?'

'I'll add it to the list.'

'What list?'

'The list of things you don't like.'

'Ah, that list.' Marikka glared at him, his eyes glinted in the moonlight. 'You think I'm spoiled. Don't you.'

Mika said nothing. She focused on not getting sea sick and avoiding looking at the sack that was dripping blood. She wondered if there was an animal in there. It was heavy enough. She didn't like this situation one bit. The guys who had brought it were criminals. What exactly was in this sack? What if it was a rare breed or something, or … She was letting her imagination run away with her. She just had to accept that this was a routine fish-feeding exercise.

TWENTY

A SILVER TRACE

Things weren't going well in the search for Marikka. Another day wasted, only one man had seen her and he seemed very reluctant to help. Mr Cole looked quite upset that they were even there standing on his doorstep so late in the evening.

'I'm sorry, sir, but I know for a fact that Marikka's father was killed years ago in a car accident. Who are you really? And what is your business with her? She has been through so much I'd hate for her to experience more pain.'

'I *am* Leon Stillwater.' He showed Mr Cole his driving licence. 'I assure you, sir, that Marikka may have *believed* I was dead, her mother is very convincing, but as you can see I am very much alive. I will find her, with or without your help.'

Mr Cole was reluctant to accept it. 'I'd have to check with the Brigstock police…'

Leon offered him his mobile. 'Call Detective Barber. He knows I'm here. I've produced Marikka's birth certificate and they have my DNA on file to compare, when she is found. I insisted.'

Mr Cole looked at the tall pale man and the little Spanish looking girl with scars on her leg and suddenly felt enormously guilty. Was it really possible that Marikka had a living father? If so, he should be helping not hindering.

'I should have called the police. I'm sorry… I was trying to protect her.'

Leon Stillwater didn't care what he did before. 'Where is she *now*, Mr Cole?'

They were standing in his waiting room. A black faced cocker spaniel slept in a basket on the floor. Mr Cole had been taken aback when this man had turned up and claimed to be Marikka's father.

'Marikka was actually here?' Leon asked him, trying not to let his hopes rise.

'With a boy. Mika. He's been working for a man called Jackson, further along by the dunes. He's up to no good, that I can guarantee you. Then she came back this afternoon.'

'Why was she here?' Anya asked, brushing hair out of her eyes. She felt Marikka's presence, but not in this room.

Mr Cole had to sit down, he found his legs were quite shaky. 'The boy was severely injured. His legs. He'd been in a car crash. He should have gone to hospital, but he's afraid to go and Jackson won't let him. Marikka says the boy is a runaway and he doesn't want his father to find him. I sent her back with some antibiotics for him and she promised to come back here once the boy was on the mend.'

Leon frowned. 'You didn't call the police about her?'

Mr Cole shrugged. 'She's scared. She says her mother will blame her for the fire. Even if her stepfather is dead, her mother can be very vindictive. I have had dealings with her last year.'

Leon understood. He could vouch for that all right.

'I said she could come and stay with me and help with the animals until things settled down.' He looked at Leon. 'I was trying to protect her. I didn't know you existed. I know how afraid she is that social services will foster her out again. She had bad experiences before and I...'

Anya wanted to ask a question and put up her hand.

Mr Cole looked at her, puzzled at her clothes. 'Yes?'

'Can I see where she was?'

Mr Cole didn't know why she needed to see the kitchen, but led them both to the back of the house.

'Would you like some tea or coffee?' He offered, trying to recover his equilibrium.

'I want to find my daughter, Mr Cole,' Leon told him. 'But yes, tea. You're the first person who's actually seen her and we've spoken to almost everyone we could from Saltfleet to Mablethorpe.'

Mr Cole led them into his kitchen and put the kettle on. Nuisance pushed his way in and sat beside Anya looking up at her with strange attention.

Anya could feel Marikka strongly. At last she had a fix on her. It would make it easier for her to follow now.

Mr Cole was talking nervously. 'I'm sorry. I like Marikka. She's a good person. I wanted to help her. She had a terrible history with her stepfather and then there was the business of the house burning down and her getting shot.'

'Marikka's wounded?' Leon asked, even more anxious now.

Mr Cole realised that they couldn't know that. 'I treated the wound. Just a graze. That's why she ran. She was afraid. Her stepfather was not a good man; that I can tell you. I want you to know I'm on Marikka's side in this.'

Leon watched the kettle boil. 'You didn't report it?'

Mr Cole was embarrassed, he shrugged. 'I didn't want her mother to know where she was. I'm sorry. I know that's wrong. But if I reported it, the police would inform her.'

'No need to worry about her now. By now she'll know I'm looking for Marikka. She'll make herself scarce. She stole from me and ruined Marikka's childhood. I'll never forgive or forget.'

Anya was concerned however. No one had mentioned Marikka had been shot.

'We should go. She might keep moving if she's afraid.'

'Jackson won't harm her.' Mr Cole tried to reassure them. 'He's under the illusion that he's hiding out from the Government, but he hasn't harmed the boy.'

Mr Cole put tea bags into three mugs. His hands were shaking with nerves. He was deathly scared Marikka's father would report him and he'd broken so many rules for that girl.

He put the mugs on the table, going to the fridge for milk.

'Help yourself to sugar.'

'Did Marikka leave anything behind?' Anya asked as casually as she could. She was disappointed that they had found a connection to Marikka but no objects she owned. She was still elusive.

Mr Cole was about to say no when he remembered about the payment. He brought milk to the table and then opened his kitchen drawer. It was a little stiff as he tugged at it.

'She paid with this.' He pulled out a silver broach and placed it into Anya's hands. 'They haven't got any money and I know she hates not paying her way. When her stepfather owed me money she offered to work for me to pay it off. I refused, of course. It wasn't her fault he was…'

Leon cut him off. 'But she had this?'

Anya gripped the silver broach hard and flopped down on a chair to think. It wasn't as rewarding as she'd hoped when she first saw it.

'She barely touched it,' she whispered. 'The boy found it, gave it to her as a gift. She saved his life.'

Mr Cole looked surprised. 'That's it exactly. She got him out of the car and brought him here. He might have died if she'd left him there.'

Anya ignored him.

'This was a present to a woman called Rose. She kept it a very long time. It doesn't belong here. It should go back to the sea.'

Leon looked at Anya, saw the cloud of concern on her face.

'What do you mean?'

'It's from a grave, Leon. You mustn't keep things from the dead. It belongs to them. It's from a drowned world.'

Mr Cole nodded, amazed at the girl's gifts. 'That would be Bonfleet. The coastline used to be a few miles further out to sea about eighty years ago. I often see bits and pieces wash up on our beaches from the town. It was flooded and left to rot. Too hard to defend. Marikka and I were talking about it earlier in fact. Jackson claims to have been raised there, but that would be impossible of course.'

Anya put the broach into her pocket. 'It must go back to the sea.'

Mr Cole raised his hands in surrender. 'By all means take it. I was going to give it back to Marikka when she returned.' He looked at Anya more closely.

'That's some gift you have, my dear.'

Anya barely acknowledged him, she wasn't used to compliments.

'Anya is helping me find Marikka and then I'll help her find her father.'

Anya looked up at Leon with surprise. It had never been part of the deal, but she heard real sincerity in his voice. She said nothing more, but hoped it was true.

'Where does Jackson live?' Anya asked as she sipped her hot tea.

'The old bomber base. It's a good long walk from here.'

'Where is it?' Leon asked, impatient to go now. He blew on his tea to cool it some, sipping it slowly.

Mr Cole pointed. 'There's a track running along behind the dunes. Are you walking?'

'No. We're on a motorbike.

'Then watch out for potholes. It's treacherous.'

Leon stood up, he had no time for the hot tea now. He shook Mr Cole's hand. 'I thank you for looking out for Marikka. You took a risk for her and I know you meant to protect her. I just hope she's still there.'

Mr Cole led the way back along the corridor.

Anya followed them out. She halted in the porch, her hands inadvertently touching the hanging wind-chimes. They spoke to her immediately.

'Your wife misses you very much, Mr Cole. She waits by the roses.'

Mr Cole stared opened-mouthed as Leon and Anya departed. He shut the door on them and frowned. No one but him knew that his wife's ashes were scattered by the roses at the base of the dunes. That was why he lived here now, to be close to his wife.

Outside the wind-chimes tinkled as if to confirm her statement. His wife had hung them there, she'd loved the sound they made in the breeze.

Had he done right by Marikka? Was he going to get into trouble for helping her? Nuisance arrived by his feet and wanted to go outside. Mr Cole followed him. How strange was that girl? How had she known so much about the broach?

The breeze blew his grey hair about his face and he felt suddenly much older than his sixty years

TWENTY-ONE

BETRAYAL

They were approaching the reef area. It was cold and the beginnings of a sea mist rose off the surface. It looked like any other stretch of open sea to Marikka, but Jackson was slowing and Mika had his compass out and was looking back at the shore – invisible in the darkness. The buoy with the bell was floating nearby, a slow flashing red light was all there was to announce the presence of shallow water.

'We're here?' Marikka asked, as huge waves rolled under them pitching them high and low.

'Yeah.'

'I'm freezing. You must be too, Mika.'

Mika nodded. 'Come on, let's get this cage off the back. I want to start back before the fog comes.'

He started to drag it to the rear of the pontoon and the pontoon immediately began to dip into the waves.

Marikka approached the cage just as the moon emerged from behind a cloud and she saw something, let out a piercing scream.

'The sack. *It moved*. Mika it moved.'

Mika had seen it too, but it was too late, the wire cage was already tipping over into the sea.

Marikka was trying to reach the sack to unhook it and sure enough, her weight just pushed it towards the water even faster. There was no way she could prevent herself from going into the sea with it.

'Mika!' She screamed.

Mika had no choice but to jump in after her. The cage would sink instantly, as it was designed to do. Marikka went down with it, still trying to rip the sack from the hook with her bare hands.

It was totally dark under the water. Marikka, her lungs straining, had managed to tear the sack open and thought she had hold of fingers, *human fingers*. But the whole cage was plunging down to the sea bed rapidly. She lost contact as her breath gave out.

Mika gripped her around the waist and dragged her back up to the surface.

'Don't be stupid. You can't do anything.' He yelled as they broke the waves.

'There's someone in the sack,' Marikka screamed at him. 'They're alive. They're alive.'

She tried to break free, but Mika wouldn't let her go. He knew there was nothing they could do. Even finding the sack in the blackness below would be impossible.

'You can't do anything,' Mika shouted at her. 'It's gone.'

Marikka was hysterical now and bit him, breaking free and trying to dive down after the cage. Mika yelled with the pain and let her go. He turned around to try and locate the pontoon and discovered that Jackson had cut it free. He'd already vanished. Jackson had abandoned them four miles out to sea.

'Jackson,' he screamed hysterically. 'Jackson, come back. Jackson, you bastard. Come back.'

He couldn't even hear the motor. Jackson must have cut the tow rope the moment they got out to the reef. They had been too busy getting the cage into the water to notice.

Marikka came up ten feet away from him, gasping for air.

She was in shock, looking around for Jackson with growing panic. 'Where is he? Where is he? Jackson?'

Only slowly did she understand that Jackson had abandoned them. Ahead of her Mika was desperately trying to reach the pontoon, moving rapidly away from them.

'Mika!'

'Come this way. Swim towards me now. The bastard cut us loose.'

Marikka was freezing cold, short of breath and desperately aware that she could die out here. She began to swim, desperately trying to blot out the sack from her mind. Who or why they had been in there was irrelevant now. She had to save herself.

Mika reached the pontoon and hauled himself up the slippery side. His mind was racing in all directions. Jackson knew what he was doing. No one knew they were out here and without sails or oars they were helpless in the current.

Marikka was at the edge of the pontoon now, already exhausted. 'I can't…'

Mika grabbed her and fell backwards whilst hauling her out of the water. They both lay there wet, freezing cold and in shock, their thoughts racing as the reality of their situation hit them.

'You bit me.' Mika complained, rubbing his hand.

'You wouldn't let me save him.'

'Him?'

'Whoever. Him or her. There was a person in the sack, Mika. A person!'

Marikka tried to picture it, but all she could remember was a slimy long fleshy thing with a fingers on the end of it. 'It had to be a person in the sack.' She suddenly remembered all those headlines about little Mollie Pendleton. She closed her eyes. Was that whose fingers she had felt? Little Mollie had been in that sack? She felt sick. She and Mika had killed her. Her head was going to burst. Jackson and the men from Brigstock were kidnappers. This whole fish feeding thing was a cover for disposing of the bodies.

Mika didn't say anything. He examined where she'd bitten him, but couldn't see any blood, at least. He didn't blame her. He was the stupid one for just accepting that this was 'fish food'.

'Jackson knew,' he said. 'He must have known. I can't believe this. We're as good as dead.'

Mika was in a total daze at the enormity of their situation.

'Say something Mika. Say something. Tell me you know how to get us back.' She shook him and Mika turned to look at her as if seeing her for the first time. She could see him suddenly come awake.

'Take off your clothes. Wring them out. There's some old spare t-shirts in the locker. We'll get sick if we sit around in wet clothes.'

'And the spin dryer? What do you think is going to dry them?'

Mika had no answer for that, but he began to strip off. Marikka turned her back to him and reluctantly did the same.

'If the person in the sack was chopped up, how come it twitched?' Marikka asked suddenly. 'I don't understand how it twitched.'

'I don't know, but they definitely couldn't have been alive. Couldn't have been.'

Marikka wasn't convinced. She was worried now that they were accessory to murder. They had tipped little Mollie into the sea in a sack, and whatever chances she'd had in life instantly had been lost. She'd never forget this. Never. She hadn't saved anyone. All she could see in her head was a chopped up Mollie in a sack. She'd have nightmares forever.

Mika was shaking and it wasn't the cold. He was thinking about other sacks, many other sacks. This wasn't the first.

She opened the locker and took out a pile of grease stained t-shirts. She threw two to Mika and kept a couple for herself. She'd look ridiculous but she was past caring about that.

'How many, Mika? How many of these special deliveries have there been? Are you even here? How many times have you been out here?

Mika didn't answer. He didn't even put the t-shirts on, even though he was freezing cold.

She shook him again. 'Mika! Wake up. Put the t-shirts on now.'

Mika silently snatched up the tops and pulled them on.

'I can't believe he left us.'

'Of course he left us. He's feeding us to the fishes. It's all my fault. Those bastards know I saw them at the fire. Of course they want me gone.'

Mika busied himself wringing out the sweaters and laying out their clothes so they would dry out. Marikka let him do it, she could see he was upset. She was calmer now, more rational. The sack probably hadn't twitched. It was just swaying on the hook. The girl in the sack *had* to be dead. If you cut a person into pieces to fit into a sack, they aren't exactly going to be alive. She couldn't have saved anyone; she knew that now. She suddenly remembered her stepfather's fatal words 'they can make anyone disappear – even you, Maggot.'

'We're four miles from land, you said. How can we get back? You know these waters. What do we do?'

Mika didn't reply. All he knew was that Jackson had repeatedly told him that the currents were lethal around here and that if he ever got stranded he'd never be seen again.

'The current...' he said.

'It's strong, I know. But what do we do?'

He remembered the weather forecast. A cold front, then fog. 'I don't know. I don't know.'

Marikka took a deep breath. Mika was as much in shock as she was, she could see that. He'd invested a lot in Jackson, swallowed a lot of his lies and he was feeling betrayed. She'd been there. She knew that feeling. She knew it hurt.

'He's not coming back for you, Mika. We're abandoned. You understand? You need to think now. I'm relying on you. There has to be a way out of this.'

He felt sick. Jackson had stolen everything from him. Trust. Faith. A whole year they had been together and he'd worked his guts out for the man, for nothing. The man had just cut him loose. How could he do that?

'The point. If we're lucky we'll end up at the point,' he said quietly.

'And if we aren't lucky?'

He didn't answer that.

'Can we steer this thing? Any paddles by any chance?'

Mika shook his head. Worse, in about fifteen hours it would deflate. They would drown for sure.

'I'm sorry, Marikka.'

'You will be if you don't start thinking. Come on. You're starfish boy genius remember. There has to be something we can do. We can't swim it. At least I can't. I was never good at swimming. There has to be something.'

'Twenty-five.'

'Twenty-five?'

'That's how many special night trips Jackson made with the sacks. Always after those men came.'

Marikka suddenly understood what was spooking him. She was horrified.

'Twenty-five people?'

'I didn't know they were people. It was supposed to be fish food...'

'They murdered this girl. Chopped her up.'

'You don't know who... Jackson didn't...' Mika said shivering.

'No? He's just the man who makes people disappear. Who was that person in the sack? What did she ever do to anyone? She was kidnapped, Mika. They got the money and killed her anyway. This is going to haunt me forever.'

Mika chewed on his lower lip. He just couldn't believe this had been going on and he never noticed a thing.

'My stepfather said those guys in Brigstock could make anyone vanish,' Marikka said quietly. 'They kidnap kids, get the money, then make them disappear.'

'Kidnappers?' Mika asked.

'Why don't they give the kids back?' Marikka asked. 'Why chop them up?'

Mika had no idea why.

Marikka leaned over the side and put her face into the cold sea to keep awake. To wash away the pain she felt for little Mollie. She rolled back and shook the water from her face and hair. 'I'm never going to sleep again. I'll have nightmares forever. Absolutely forever.'

She glanced across at Mika and sensed he felt guilty all this had taken place under his nose. 'Don't beat yourself up about this, Mika. You couldn't have saved any of them. You know that, right? No one will blame you.'

Mika didn't say anything. Marikka looked out across the darkness.

'Concentrate. We have to save ourselves right now. Get us out of this. There *has* to be a way to get back to shore'

'We're drifting south.' Mika said eventually.

'And?'

'And nothing. We're drifting south, that's all.'

'Mika. Tell me straight. Are we going to survive this?'

Mika chewed on his bottom lip, felt the cold rising fog on his face, considered that they had no oars, little drinking water, no lifejackets, no shelter. Drowning would have been an easier option.

'You want the truth?' He whispered.

'No.'

TWENTY-TWO

THE HANGAR

'We're closer now. I know we are,' Leon said. He was disappointed but didn't want to admit it. He'd expected to find Marikka here.

The hangar was abandoned. No one was home. The door wasn't even locked.

Anya walked towards the dock. She sensed Marikka was everywhere, but nowhere, the boy too. She could feel they had been here very recently.

Leon went inside the hangar. It stank of diesel, but clearly people had been living here. There was a milk carton with an expiry date two days before on a counter. He saw bloodied bandages lying on an unmade bed. The boy had been injured the vet had said. He picked up a leaflet stained with a coffee cup ring mark.

Bonfleet Reef Fish Sanctuary.
Jackson Reef Enterprises is developing an endangered fish safe breeding environment in the shallow waters of Bonfleet. Applications have been made to the EU Fisheries Commission to make this a No-Fishing zone in perpetuity. Donations to…

The map showed a highlighted area off the coast.

He went to the door and called out to Anya. 'She was staying here. I know it.'

Anya was standing at the dock, an inflatable was moored there, a rope trailing from the stern. She leant down and touched the rope. She felt a series of flashing images, but couldn't make sense of them. She knew this rope had been cut deliberately in an act of vengeance. Someone had meant to kill somebody.

'Leon? Marikka's in trouble.' She closed her eyes, she could feel evil all around her.

Leon was at her side already. He saw the boat, he had the leaflet in his hand as he looked out to sea.

'This rope cut... bad thoughts, Leon.' Anya said, her eyes half closed as she sought the truth and shuddered.

Leon handed her the leaflet and Anya's eyes widened and looked up at him.

'Fish sanctuary?'

'But on top of the water or at the bottom?' Leon said tersely. 'That's the question.'

He climbed into the boat and checked the fuel tank; it was near empty. 'You see any fuel store nearby?'

Anya looked both ways. She was familiar with boats and their need for fuel. She had an image in her head of a dirty fuel tank hidden behind a tall bushy purple buddleia and pointed behind her. Leon followed the direction, and discovered the fuel tank and a fuel can behind the overgrown bushes.

'Well done.'

Anya was looking out across the waves with a worried frown on her face. She had never been out on the open sea, quite a contrast to the calm stillness of the canals. 'It's going to be rough.'

'You can stay.'

'I'm not staying here. This is an evil place.'

Leon filled the five-litre can, looking back at the hangar and the scrap metal left discarded everywhere.

There was no order here, no sense of a real business. A strange place for his daughter to end up. A fish sanctuary? Who were they kidding?

'I'm going to look for lifejackets,' Anya told him, running towards the hangar. She didn't tell him what she feared most was that they were going to find floating bodies. There was a strange distinct smell of death here. She hated this place.

Leon had filled the tank and refilled the can in case they needed longer time on the water. He got the engine started by the time Anya returned with old and tatty lifejackets, they'd be better than nothing. She threw some blankets onto the boat as well.

'In case they're cold.' She said. But feared they'd need them to wrap the bodies with. She had a dreadful feeling that time and luck was running out.

'We might not find them,' Leon said. He pushed them away from the dock and hauled the severed tow rope in.

'There's still hope,' Anya whispered quietly.

TWENTY-THREE

BELGIUM

'No one but Jackson knows we're out here and he's not exactly going to alert the coastguard.' Marikka said quietly. She was only now beginning to see how bleak their prospects were of surviving this. She understood that Mika had figured this out from the first moment Jackson had abandoned them.

It was no wonder Jackson hadn't wanted her to join them in the hangar. Mika had trusted him and clearly hadn't ever questioned anything.

'I'm sorry, Mika. This is all my fault.'

'No. I know he's mean. I knew the moment I hurt my legs he'd wanted me gone. He's …'

'Mean.'

'Yeah. But what the hell are we going to do?' He lay down on the pontoon sensing the current was picking up speed beneath them. The breeze was steadily pushing them ever further out to sea. 'We're headed towards the point,' he added. 'We could swim for it, if we get closer. If we even see it. It's about thirty miles from here.'

Marikka scowled. She hated feeling so helpless.

'What speed are we doing?'

'Five, six knots maybe. It's gone midnight now.'

She did a quick calculation. 'So we'd be there around four or five in the morning. It'll still be dark.'

'We have to stay awake.'

'What comes after the point?' Marikka asked.

Mika shrugged. 'We could end up anywhere.'

'Not anywhere, Mika. Will the current take us further out to sea or further down the coast?'

Mika didn't reply. Marikka was conscious that she was only making it worse. She sighed and reached out to him squeezing his shoulder.

'I don't suppose you brought a pack of cards?'

'I've got a lucky stone?' He whispered.

'It had better be very lucky.'

'I keep it on me all the time.' Mika said, turning to look at her.

'Well, I guess it must work. I can't believe you're alive at all the way you drive.'

He grinned. 'See? It works.'

'I was joking.'

'Oh.' His face fell.

She relented. 'Right. We have to stay awake all night.' She tried to think of something that would get his mind working. 'Tell me the name of every World Champion Grand Prix driver, ever.'

Mika stared at her with surprise. 'Serious?'

'You don't know? I thought you took motor-racing seriously.' She teased.

'I do know.'

'As if.' She watched him concentrate for a moment.

'Farina, Fangio, Ascari twice, then Fangio four times, Hawthorn, Brabham…'

Marikka stared at him with surprise. He really did know.

'God no, stop already, or I'll tell you the names of all of the Horse Championship riders and we'd need a whole month on this raft.'

Mika fell silent peeved she'd stopped him mid-flow.

'I'm sorry,' she said after a few minutes of awkward silence. She knew she'd upset him. 'I don't really like lists. And actually I don't know the names of *any* of the horse trial champions.'

He replied after a couple of minutes annoyed that he couldn't actually remember who was world champion in 1981.

'I've seen them riding on the beach with their poncy black helmets on. They never say hello.'

'I would have said hello. To be honest, I loved riding Monday, but

I hated dressage, that crappy tight jacket and tying your hair under the stupid riding helmet stuff. There's so many rules. And everyone is so bitchy to one another. It's not good for the horse either, I swear it. Horses just want to run free and dance in the wind. Making them jump like that is cruel. I didn't know that last year, but I swear I believe it now.'

'Do you think we change much as we grow up?' Mika asked a moment later, feeling the chills now. He was shaking.

Marikka didn't reply immediately. It was obvious wasn't it. Everyone changes. But then again. She looked across at him and softened a little.

'Not you. Mika will be the guy who fixes the big problem that saves the race and makes the driver the hero.'

'Now you're mocking me.'

'You didn't ever want to be the driver?'

'You've seen my driving.'

'All you needed was brakes.'

Mika laughed, but stopped when a huge waved passed under them and slapped them down hard, before another wave slid under.

'Uh-oh.'

'What?'

'I think we're further out than I thought,' he said.

'Is that bad?'

'Didn't you want to see Belgium and all that chocolate?'

'Could be interesting.'

'If we don't drown or die of thirst.'

'How long does it take to die of thirst?'

'I never tried it.'

'One day? Two? Three?'

'We can't drink seawater. I know that.'

'Or your pee. I saw a movie when a man had to do that to stay alive.'

'Eww. Did he survive?'

'No.'

'We've got two half-litres of water and three packets of Saltines,' Mika said looking at the provisions. 'I don't think we should eat the salty biscuits even if we're starving.'

'Don't even talk about them, even knowing they're there makes me thirsty.'

'I need to pee though.'

'Eww.'

'You'll need to eventually. Turn your back,' Mika said.

'I'm never going to pee and don't rock the pontoon.'

'I'm not rocking it.' Mika stood up, hoping he wouldn't topple over into the water. He felt dizzy and trying to stand still on a pontoon going up and down all the time was difficult.

Marikka was scared to fall asleep. She knew that bloody sack would haunt her dreams. Chocolate. Think of chocolate instead she told herself.

Belgium. How long would it take to get to Belgium?

TWENTY-FOUR

ALL AT SEA

Marikka glimpsed the stars and wondered which one was the abandoned space station destined to circle the earth until one day it would hurtle to the ground and land on some unfortunate city.

'You think our parents ever thought about us before we were born?'

Mika opened one eye, he'd been trying to stay awake but was struggling. 'No.'

'I would think about the world, the state of the planet, the weather. I would think about it and wonder if I could always look after him or keep him safe.' Marikka said.

'You'd never have kids. No one who ever thought about it had kids, that's why everything is so messed up.' Mika told her.

'Thinking parents don't have kids?'

'Nah.'

'My mother never thinks about anything except how she looks, or if anyone is looking at her,' Marikka said. She wondering where she was now and what lies she was telling about her wayward daughter.

Mika tried to remember what his mother looked like, but saw only a flash of curses and bruises from his Dad and his mother cowering behind her hands in the kitchen.

'Try to sleep,' he told her, coughing.

'You're crazy. One of us has to stay awake.'

'And do what? This'll go wherever it wants.'

'You're very...'

'Yeah, I am.'

Marikka smiled. Mika was a very strange boy. She stared at the sky again as the raft rose and fell with the waves.

Mika could smell burning. He sat up on his haunches and gazed towards the shore.

'That look natural to you?'

Marikka had smelled it too. She was looking at what had to be a major fire on the shore. 'Farmers burning stubble in the fields after harvest probably. They aren't supposed to but…'

'Looks more like a forest.' Mika said.

'I didn't think there were any forests around here.'

'Yeah, you're right. Fields. I hadn't thought of stubble.'

'Or a pier. Maybe Scarness pier.'

'Scarness pier burned down three years ago.'

'I used to love going there. Candy floss and the big dipper.'

Mika had different memories of Scarness. Getting beaten about the head by his father when he was drunk. Having to sleep on the beach because his father had lost the hotel money on the horses.

'You know that Jackson was just exploiting you,' Marikka said suddenly.

Mika shrugged. He knew what Jackson was, but Marikka had only just run away from home. She didn't know what it was like sleeping rough for weeks on end, begging for food from people who swore at you because you were dirty.

'It was a place to stay. He needed someone to do stuff.'

Marikka detected the sadness in Mika's voice and didn't press it.

'Can you do anything?' Mika asked. 'I mean, aside from …'

'Besides saving boys from their own stupidity.'

Mika reddened. He'd asked for that. 'I meant…'

'I know what you meant.'

'If you want to survive you have to be able to do stuff, stuff that other people don't want to do.'

Marikka sighed. Mika was right. What skills did she have? She could always be a stable girl; she knew she was good with horses. She could teach Mika how to do it quickly enough. There was usually a warm place to sleep on a farm.

'We'll find a place somewhere, OK? Plenty of horses Newmarket way. We could try around there. And thanks,' Marikka added.

'For what?'

'For making me think about what we should be doing.'

Mika didn't reply. He hadn't thought much about his life with Jackson until she'd turned up, but he knew that he should have left earlier. A lot earlier. He still couldn't believe he'd cut them adrift. Or that he was involved with those murderers.

Marikka remembered Mika needed to take another pill. Luckily she still had them in her jeans pocket and the tiny plastic tube had survived the dunking. She popped one out.

'Here. You need to take this.'

Mika looked over at her and made a face.

'No point. Might be dead by morning.'

Marikka stared at him, anger flaring.

'You can stop thinking like that now, all right? You're taking this pill and you're going to get better and **we** are going survive. Don't you give up so easily. I'm not giving up. Understand?'

Mika reluctantly took the pill and put it in his mouth. He uncapped the water bottle and took a swig, swallowing.

'I swallowed it. OK? You don't know the sea. We're lucky it's not rough. We would have drowned already, probably.'

'But we haven't. Don't wish for trouble, alright?'

Mika lay back down - he had a headache again and his temperature was rising. The bandages around his legs had come loose and were still soggy. He unwrapped them, let them pool beside him.

Marikka forced herself to stay awake. She didn't know how, but she was determined to survive this. She refused to believe that this was all her life amounted to. She wished Deacon was with them. He was a stronger swimmer than her. Half of her was missing now he was gone. He'd never been 'just a dog'. It was as if her shadow had died.

They drifted some more. Mika was restless beside her and she knew he must be hurting.

'You know you have to go to school again, don't you.' Marikka said a few minutes later.

'I'm going to apprentice to Mclaren.' Mika said quietly.

'McLaren?'

'You're such a girl. McLaren, only the world's greatest motor racing team. Well used to be.'

Marikka stared at him for a second. 'That McLaren. Wow, that's really ambitious.'

'They only take the best.' Mika said proudly.

'But wouldn't you need qualifications?'

'I know engines. I know electronics.' Mika said.

Marikka shook her head. 'Sometimes life isn't about how good you are. It's all about the stupid bits of paper you have to have.'

'I'm going down the apprentice route. I'll get there. You'll see.'

'I never met a boy who knew what he wanted to do before. No one thinks about careers in Brigstock. My father, my real father, once asked me what I wanted to be and I told him a Judge.'

'A Judge?' Mika laughed. 'What with a wig and stuff?'

Marikka smiled. She didn't mind that he'd laughed. 'I had no idea what a Judge did or anything. I think I meant lawyer. Who knows what a kid thinks.'

'And now?'

Marikka frowned. 'I wanted to run a school, one where kids would actually want to go and learn useful stuff, then have long breaks where we'd go riding or sailing or whatever. The kids would say what they wanted to learn and we'd bring in experts to teach us. No teachers. Just people with skills and we'd learn from them. No one would ever be afraid of being smart or ambitious or wrong, and there'd definitely be no bullies. They'd be excluded on the spot.'

Mika stared at her in wonder. 'Sounds cool. I'd go. You should definitely start it.'

'You think?'

'Definitely. Not that I've ever been to school much.'

'I hate being fifteen,' Marikka sighed. 'Got no rights over my own life. That's something else I want to change.'

'I need to sleep,' Mika said with a yawn.

Marikka curled up beside him for warmth.

TWENTY-FIVE

MR COLE MAKES A CALL

Detective Barber stood by the dock as Mr Cole walked over, his dog Nuisance at his heels. He could think of better places to be at five in the morning.

'You the man who phoned?'

Mr Cole nodded, turning up his collar against the early morning chill.

'There's no one here.' The Detective pointed out. He was annoyed he'd been called out. Just his bad luck he was on the night shift and they'd caught him just before he went off duty. A uniform cop was looking around, shining his torch across the debris strewn patch of land in front of the hangar.

'A man called Stillwater came to see me late last night. He was looking for his daughter Marikka.'

'So you said on the phone. But she's not here.'

Mr Cole indicated the motorbike left beside the hangar.

'Mr Stillwater had a motorbike. I'm worried because there's a sick boy supposed to be here. Mr Stillwater wouldn't just abandon his motor cycle, Detective.'

Detective Barber looked at the small dock, empty of water now that the tide had receded.

'I'm not sure what you're saying, Mr Cole.'

'There was a man here, Jackson.' He handed over one of the fishing sanctuary leaflets to the cop. 'The boy was living here. Marikka was looking after him. He'd had an accident. I was going to call you because she was going to come and stay with me and...'

'What's your relationship to the girl?'

'I was her vet. She used to have a horse. I've known her about two

147

or three years.'

Detective Barber wasn't aware of any horse.

'We're talking about Marikka Stander, right? You know we're looking for her?'

'I know her stepfather burned the house down and died after he tried to shoot her.'

'Is that what she told you?'

'I saw her wounds, Detective. She's lucky she wasn't killed and very afraid. Her mother will say she did it and she doesn't know how to defend herself.'

'You are opening yourself up to needing some defence yourself, Mr Cole. Where is Marikka now?'

'I think this man Jackson has done something bad. I think we should be looking out there.' He pointed to the open water. 'I've got no proof, but if I was you, I'd be looking more closely at this fish sanctuary.'

Detective Barber looked at the sea. 'There's nothing I can do about that. Outside my jurisdiction.'

Mr Cole shook his head. 'We should do something. If Mr Stillwater's gone out there.'

'Then, someone is doing something.' Detective Barber remarked drily. 'We've got nothing here.'

A shout went up from the police officer inspecting the dock.

'Got some fresh blood here, sir.'

Detective Barber swore. He'd have to do something now.

TWENTY-SIX

WINDMILLS

'What's that noise?' Marikka asked suddenly, shaking sleep from her head and sitting up, shivering. She been fast asleep, her neck was stiff and sore. A cold mist had come up from nowhere and surrounded them.

'Huh?'

'That weird whooshing noise. Can't you hear it?'

Mika listened. It wasn't regular, but now he concentrated he could hear it, but not the direction it was coming from in the mist.

'Not a boat engine,' he said, not sure if he was trying to reassure himself or Marikka.

Marikka stared into the rising mist with growing concern. If they were going to collide with something she wanted to see it first. She had visions of some great ocean liner bearing down on them.

'It's getting louder.'

Mika sat up, feeling his head, heavy and throbbing now. His legs hurt like hell and he wondered if he should put them into the water to cool them down.

'Much closer,' Marikka was saying.

Strange shapes loomed ever closer, as if they had wandered into a forest. Yet what kind of forest grew in the sea?

A breeze blew the mist that swirled in dense clouds around them, freezing cold ghost breaths that felt clammy around their faces. Above them now the noise grew ever louder with an eerie intensity. They passed really close to a towering tree and suddenly Marikka understood.

'Wind turbines!'

Mika looked up and could just make out the swish as a turbine blade turned high above their heads. He realised with a chilling horror that they had drifted much further out than he'd thought and they might be off Scarness or worse, even further along as far as the Swanage Turbine Forest off the Norfolk coast.

'My god there has to be hundreds of them,' Marikka was saying, as the mist momentarily parted. She glimpsed a fantastic row of turbines stretching way off into the distance.

'A thousand.' Mika informed her. He didn't want to tell her how far they'd drifted from the mainland.

'Does anyone maintain them? Is there someone out here?' Marikka asked; hope rising in her voice.

Mika shook his head. 'It's automatic.'

Marikka pulled a face. 'Is it safe? For us I mean. Electromagnetic waves or something we can't see? My real Dad always used to go on about telephone masts and how dangerous they are. Wouldn't live near one.'

'They're just generating electricity for the mainland. That's all.'

They passed many more, few turning at all in the mist.

'God I'm freezing now.' Marikka whispered.

'I'm boiling. Stick close to me,' Mika said, although he did wonder if he was going to pass some lethal bug on to Marikka now he was sick.

Marikka huddled closer. Looking back at the metal forest.

'What happens when they go wrong?'

'They send a boat out. I've seen a special barge carrying the blades. They ship them from Hull. They're huge. Really huge.'

They fell silent as they drifted through the metal forest listening to the few blades whooshing in the mist above them. Both were wondering how deep these ghostly trees were and how long it had taken to build this forest out here. Mika began to despair. They were definitely going further out to sea. Rescue was looking more and more unlikely.

TWENTY-SEVEN

JACKSON'S REEF

Leon circled the buoy one last time. He knew he'd found the right place. Shone his torch on the buoy. Someone had crudely painted 'Jackson's Reef' on the side of it. But of his daughter and the boy, there was no sign at all.

Anya wasn't well. She had never been at sea before and hated the motion of the swell and the breeze that lashed her hair against her face.

'We'll have to go back,' Leon said, sensing defeat.

Even though Anya was green and knew she'd be sick she shook her head.

'Head south, Leon. Follow the current. I know they're still alive. I just know it.'

Leon wanted to believe her, he really did, but he wasn't sure he should let his heart rule his head. 'The North Sea is a big place, Anya. They're drifting, we might never find them.'

She looked at him and narrowed her eyes. She pointed. 'Go south. Now. We'll find them. I know we will.'

Leon turned the boat and headed south. Pleased he'd brought the spare five-litre can of fuel. They could still do a few more hours before needing to head back.

Anya suddenly leant over the side and heaved. She made a terrible noise, then did it all over again. She hated the sea. Never wanted to live on water ever again as long as she lived.

'Better out than in,' Leon reassured her.

Anya tried to smile, but then turned and spewed again.

Leon looked ahead at the wide expanse of the sea. A mist was coming up. He knew they were running out of time. The night was receding. Dawn in an hour. He had no signal on his phone and was strongly aware that they could be lost to the sea if he wasn't careful. He kept the coast to his right, which was rapidly disappearing from view now in the mist. He wished he had flares. Wished he'd brought a lot of things with him. He didn't know if the current would have taken his daughter further out to sea or towards the land. He knew nothing. All he had was Anya who was flying on instinct.

Around them the mist swirled, slowly intensifying. He sensed they'd soon lose the ability to know north from south if the mist thickened any more. He prayed for a strong breeze. He prayed for Marikka. 'Keep her safe. Whatever you do, or how this turns out between her and me – just keep her safe- please.'

TWENTY-EIGHT

AN ISLAND OF HOPE

She glanced up at the shriek of seabirds. It was the late morning as far she could make out. The mist still swirled all around them, but at least it was moving. A breeze was pushing them along faster and the steady rhythm of the waves rolling beneath them was making Marikka drowsy. Mika was sound asleep next to her, burning up, his face red and sweaty. Jackson would be far away by now. She sent evil thoughts back across the waves towards him. It wouldn't help, but it did make her feel better.

If there were birds, then… she saw something. Thought it might be a ship. Ships were supposed to have lights on in mist – so it had to be something else, but what else could it be out here? A ghost ship? That would be handy at least.

'Mik?'

He didn't stir. Marikka sat up and stared into the gloom, seawater splashing onto the pontoon as the waves seemed to change direction somehow. Another bird shrieked. She knew what that meant. They had something to perch on here. Something close that she just couldn't see in the mist.

'Mika.' She prodded him awake. He stirred slightly.

'Mika there's something out there. It's huge. I know it is. It's massive. Mik, wake up. Wake up now!'

Mika sat up, sweating, still caught up in a strange dream where his mother was standing in the living room at home folding sheets and telling him that…

'Wake up. Help me paddle, we have to move towards it or we'll miss it.'

Mika stared into the gloom, shaking off the dream and understood immediately what it was. 'It's the old gas rig. I know where we are. We're past Scarness.'

He didn't explain more. He just slipped off the side of the pontoon into the sea shouting with shock at the cold, then began to kick out, pushing the pontoon towards the giant platform.

'Stand up, stand up. Grab it, grab something as we go by.'

Marikka didn't have to be told. The sound of the birds shrieking overhead was loud in their ears now. She stood uncertainly as they moved closer and closer to the metal structure. It stood on huge rusted legs anchored to the sea floor.

'Left Mika, push left.'

He shifted position and kicked them left. Only now was he aware of just how bad he felt, how weak his legs were. This wasn't him. He hated being weak.

Marikka looked around for something to tie them to the leg.

'The tow rope,' Mika called out.

She remembered what side it was on and jumped on it, hauling it in from the sea. It was cold and slimy but she had the presence of mind to measure it as she pulled it in, sea water pooling at her toes. 'Nine metres, I think.'

But as they drew closer to the giant steel leg she sensed it wasn't long enough. Not by a long shot.

'What's the circumference of the leg do you think?'

Mika frowned. 'Too big. Can you see anything to anchor us at all? A loop, a ring or...'

Marikka was feeling the cold slimy steel leg now, it was covered in seaweed and barnacles, but she couldn't see anything to tie the rope to. She was getting scared now that they'd slip by this thing, and be lost forever. Marikka anxiously searched for an access ladder. Each leg was equally huge in diameter all covered in seaweed or sea creatures to the high tide level. Above them, way above them, she could make out the gas platform safe from the sea and anything drifting underneath.

'You think there's anyone up there?' She asked.

'Nah. It was abandoned when the gas ran out. Jackson said it was too expensive to remove or they went bankrupt or something.'

'Are we at high or low tide?'

Mika thought about it a moment. 'Incoming tide I think, that's good. We'll rise with the sea.' He was beginning to feel hope again despite being freezing cold.

Marikka was staring at the top half of the leg. 'Mik, I see some metal rails. Look up past the seaweed.'

Mika saw where she was pointing. The rails came down to about twenty or so feet above them. An escape route of some kind, it meant there was a definite way to the top if they could get there. 'We have to keep the pontoon pinned here until the tide brings us up the leg.' Mika said.

Marikka had already figured that out. She looked at each leg once again more carefully. There had to be something they could tie up to.

'Wait. Give me the rope.' Mika asked. Marikka passed down the end to him. 'Keep the pontoon steady, OK? Don't drift away from the leg.'

Marikka did as she was told, trying to grip the tufts of seaweed growing on the steel leg as huge rolling waves passed under them, nearly unbalancing her. She watched Mika swim out to the centre dragging the rope with him and wondered what he was going to do. He suddenly took a deep breath and dived down.

Marikka watched anxiously, desperate to hold station, but feeling the pontoon being pulled by the different currents.

He was gone for ages.

'Mika?' She began to panic. How long could a boy hold his breath underwater?

'Mika?' She screamed.

He appeared unexpectedly to the right of her, desperately sucking in air. 'Help me.'

All his energy was spent. It took all of his strength to get back on board, even with Marikka helping. She could feel how desperately cold he was.

'Tied it to a metal strut. It'll keep us here,' he gasped.

Marikka pulled off his wet clothes and rubbed him down to revive him as he shivered uncontrollably. She made him wear one of her own warm t-shirts. She held him tight, cradled him in her arms and he fell asleep instantly. His stitches were red raw and probably infected. She prayed the salt water had the miracle properties he believed they had. He was going to need them.

Marikka held him close to keep him warm. She wondered if they'd get up that ladder and what they'd find up there. A phone, or a radio? At least, she figured, they were no longer on their way to Belgium.

TWENTY-NINE

A TRACE OF MARIKKA

'What are they?'

Leon stared into the mist and gradually a shape took places as a thrumming noise reached his ears. He finally could make sense of it. 'Wind turbines. Nothing to be afraid of. There's lots of them out in the North Sea now.'

'Are they safe?'

Leon shrugged. 'Not likely to fall over if that's what you mean, but if one of those blades falls off you'd know about it.' He shut his eyes, breathing in the mist.

'You sure they came this way, Anya?'

Anya concentrated for a moment, staring to her left. 'Yes. I'm certain.'

Leon steered the boat through an avenue of turbines, the steady whoosh of the blades faintly disturbing somewhere in the centre of his brain.

'Which way?' Leon was totally reliant of this girl now. If she was wrong he'd most likely have lost his daughter forever.

Anya pointed between the turbine masts. 'That way.'

'You can see something I can't?'

'People leave a wake. Everyone has a wake, even you. You can't see it?'

Leon smiled. 'No. I don't think there's many people who could either.'

Anya shrugged. 'We're lucky they're the only people out here besides us. You can't follow anyone in a crowd, all the colours get mixed up.'

Leon tried his best to see any signs of colours in the white mist but he saw none.

'Left a little, go the other side of the next mast. They're following the current remember.'

'You can see a difference between them?' Leon asked, curious now.

Anya nodded. 'Marikka is crimson, the boy is electric blue.'

'I envy you,' Leon told her.

'Why?'

'It's a pretty special gift.'

'You could probably see them too, if you tried.'

Leon doubted it.

'More left,' Anya barked.

'They're going further and further out to sea, ' Leon muttered, unhappy about that.

'But we're closer. The colours are stronger,' Anya added, to give him hope.

Leon was relieved to hear it as Anya dropped a hand down into the water to splash her face. She suddenly looked up at Leon.

'You think my father would ever care for me as much as you care for Marikka?'

Leon didn't know how to answer that, but he tried.

'A good father always cares, Anya. Always worries.' He hoped that was true.

THIRTY

RUST BUCKET

Climbing the wet slimy rails covered in seaweed was hard enough. It took the two of them all their combined strength to open the rusted steel hatch at the top and just when they got through it, the wind caught it and slammed it back down. It jammed. Now they were trapped.

Mika saw that they had entered an area where giant metal superstructure supported the main platform above.

'God, what is this? We're not at the top.' Marikka protested. She looked up and shuddered. 'It's so rusted. Is it safe?'

Mika smiled banging his fist on a steel beam. 'Might last a hundred years. It's strong. Don't worry.'

Some daylight came through from buckled rusted side panels as they made their way up ten flights of salt encrusted stairs. Everything was flaking and rusting. The howling wind was making spooky noises and whipped around Marikka's hair. She didn't like this place one bit.

Mika stared at the huge rusted steel beams angled up towards the vast metal floor above them. When it was built it had to take the weight of all the drilling equipment, helicopters, the crew and stay stable against all the power of the North Sea. Now it was a ghostly shell and water dripped on them from everywhere. He tried to imaging how long it had taken to build it and how many men it had needed.

'They towed this whole platform here from Scotland, y'know.'

Marikka shivered, shooting him a puzzled glance. She didn't much care where it had come from. She just concentrated on not falling and putting one foot in front of the other on slimy steel steps.

'I hope there's a door. Hell, Mika. What if we can't get out of here? God, how high is this thing?'

'Don't even think it.'

They finally came to door with a porthole in it. Mika couldn't turn the handle it was so stiff. Marikka clasped her hands over his and together, as they grunted and strained, they heard it reluctantly scrape loose and eventually turn. Marikka laughed with relief. She had genuinely thought they were trapped. With great effort she prised the door open as it protested loudly on rusted hinges.

Mika limped through first, blinking in the bright light. They were on the crew quarters deck. A passage ran alongside it, a vertical drop to the sea on one side. The seabirds had made good use of it at least, their droppings encrusted everything. The birds squawked overhead alarmed at the intrusion on their world.

It was weirdly sunny here up above the mist. Mika flopped onto the deck exhausted, as Marikka explored the weather beaten platform. It was clear that it had been abandoned many years now. Windows were broken, pools of water and oil lay everywhere, she found no sign of a working phone or flares or anything useful.

She was standing in what had to have been the accommodation quarters. Above them towered all manner of piping and further up beyond that she could see a helipad. No chopper was coming to rescue them, that was for sure.

The metal beds in the rudimentary crews quarters were still there, but no mattresses. She wrenched open a metal cupboard and to her relief found blankets. They smelled disgusting and some had moth holes but they'd keep Mika warm. There was no food, no water, no short wave radio, and no electricity. It was truly abandoned. Old newspapers filled a bin. She didn't know what language they were printed in but she could see the date. 1995.

She returned with the blankets.

Mika was drinking from a rusty can. 'Here.'

'Where did you get that?' It looked disgusting.

'Tins by the crane. It's rainwater. Won't kill you. Been living on rainwater for almost a year now.'

Marikka wasn't sure about that. Nevertheless she drank some. It wasn't as bad as she thought it would be.

'I think I could eat one of those Saltines now. I'm starving.' That's when she remembered they had left the biscuits and the water bottles back down on the pontoon. Stupid. Very.

Mika wrapped a blanket around him, grateful for the warmth. The wind was pretty brisk up this high above the sea and his clothes were still damp. He looked like a ghost his face was so white and his lips were blue. His eyes looked terrible, glassy and red. Marikka only had four pills left for him, but without food she knew it wasn't going to do him much good.

'Wrap yourself up,' he croaked. 'You have to stay warm. Can't think properly if you're cold.'

'I'm not so cold. It's your fever talking,' she told him. 'You're shivering.'

Mika nodded. Going back into the sea hadn't helped any. 'We can't afford to miss anything. A ship, a fishing boat, anything. You have to keep watching.'

'You sleep first, OK?' Marikka said. 'I'll keep watch. Curl up in the sun by the back of the cabin over there if you really have to stay outside. It's warmer.'

He nodded. He wanted to stay outside, but equally he wanted to get warm.

'How will people even see us?' Marikka asked despairingly, as she looked across the misty sea below. 'I should be on the helipad deck. We would have a 360 view from there.'

Mika frowned straining to see where she meant. When he saw the platform he couldn't immediately figure out how she'd get there. He shook his head.

'The mist will go. Always comes at this time of year. This wind will clear it. You'll see. You see anything out there, run around here with a blanket waving it in the air. Yell like hell.'

Marikka looked up at the birds who no doubt resented them arriving on their territory. Making them fly up suddenly might attract attention as well.

Mika limped towards the back of the cabin and she felt bad for him. She stared out across the sea below them and saw nothing but mist. She looked up again at the hungry birds with their huge wings and wondered what they tasted like – assuming the huge birds didn't catch her first.

She knew that they could die out here. Perhaps that's all they deserved. She thought again about little Mollie. The touch of her fingers as she'd plummeted down to the bottom of the sea. They'd done that. How do you make yourself forget such a thing. She looked at her fingers, felt her heart racing. Jackson had known all this time. Letting Mika do all that work. The whole fish sanctuary was a lie. It was just the last link in a …

She shuddered. *Have to blot it out. Have to stop thinking about Mollie. Have to save myself. Do I even deserve to be saved? Would Mollie think she deserved to be saved?* Marikka closed her eyes. *Those slimy fingers had cursed her forever.*

THIRTY-ONE

STALLED

Anya looked worried as Leon stared at the engine. It had abruptly cut out. Now they too were helplessly drifting to god knows where and she hated being on the sea that just never kept still.

'The mist is lifting.' Leon remarked. Indeed the breeze was blowing harder now and taking the mist with it.

Anya began to feel hope again. She hadn't liked to mention it at the time but as the mist had thickened she had thoughts of them being lost out here forever.

Leon was leaning over the side, pulling the outboard engine in to examine the propeller.

'Here's our problem,' he announced, glancing back at Anya with a smile.

She could see a bright orange nylon rope wrapped around the propeller that had stopped the motor.

'Luckily it's designed to cut out when this happens, otherwise I'd be looking as miserable as you right now.'

Anya tried to smile, but didn't feel like it. Leon produced a penknife from his pocket and began to hack away at the rope.

'You think that…'

Suddenly two fighter jets flying extremely low zoomed overhead towards the coast. Anya nearly fell out the boat and Leon ducked they were so low.

'Where the hell have they come from?' He shouted, his face white with shock. 'Where they hell are they going?'

Anya shook with fright. They had been so close.

THIRTY-TWO

BIRDSHOCK

Marikka had watched the jets fly over. She was practising a run with the blanket at the time and nearly fell off the platform with fright when the two jets screamed overhead towards the coast.

'Bloody bombing again. Do they do nothing else around here but bomb the beaches?'

She saw Mika's head as he'd sat up with shock at the noise.

'Don't look at me. They didn't see me. We're just lucky they didn't try to land on this thing. You were right though. The mist is clearing.'

Mika nodded. His heart was still racing. He was used to the jets coming in the early mornings or late evenings to bomb the beach, but he'd never been this close to them. It seemed to him that he could have touched one as they flew over.

Marikka was annoyed. Maybe they'd seen her, maybe they hadn't. But would they do anything about it? She made a decision. What they really needed was a fire. After all she was a firestarter right? Might as well live up to her reputation.

THIRTY-THREE

WHERE'S THERE'S SMOKE

'Smoke.' Anya suddenly shouted.

Leon was cutting the last of the rope and hoping that the engine would restart.

'What?'

'Smoke, over there, on the water.'

'It's mist. It doesn't all blow away at once.'

'No. It's smoke.'

Leon looked to where Anya was pointing. It was true. Smoke was rising, surely impossible on the water.

Anya smiled.

'It's them.'

'How do you know?'

'I know.'

Leon shrugged. He turned his attention to the engine and filled it up with the last of their fuel. He resolved to inspect the smoke but if that didn't turn out to be them; they would have to go back. They had little choice in the matter.

'Cross your fingers,' Leon told her as he pulled the cord.

It started on the second try.

'We need to hurry,' Anya told him. She didn't know why but she sensed something was wrong.

Leon headed towards the smoke. He was beginning to worry about how Marikka would react to him being alive. It would be a terrible shock for her.

Anya was studying his face. 'Don't worry. She will forgive you – eventually.'

Leon stared back at Anya. Forgive him for what? Dying, and yet not dying? For not being there for her? For never finding her? Would he forgive himself if the roles were reversed?

'Are there any islands out here?' Anya was asking.

'I don't think so.'

'But I can see one.'

Anya's eyes were sharper than his. He could only see smoke, but little else. Certainly no island.

THIRTY-FOUR

FIRESIGN

Mika woke. He was shivering. The wind had found him and the sun had disappeared below the horizon. He knew they'd lose the light soon. He could smell smoke. He sat up and rubbed his eyes. It was definitely smoke.

'Marikka?'

He stood up letting the blanket drop and walked around the corner and stared with total astonishment at the huge bonfire burning on the helipad.

Marikka had obviously found her way up there and he watched as she threw some chairs on the flames and then some other stuff that made it smoke. She was coughing as the smoke blew back over her.

Mika could barely speak. His throat was sore and swollen but he was aware of one particular thing.

'Marikka!'

'What? Come up here and get warm. There's a stairway by the big red sign. You reckon anyone can see this from the mainland yet?'

'Marikka this is a *Gas Platform*!'

Mika ran for the stairs as fast as he could, heart in his mouth, aware his legs felt like jelly.

He emerged breathless onto the helipad as Marikka heaped some old newspapers onto the flames.

'Cool huh? Not got much else to burn though'.

'So?' She answered.

'Gas, Marikka.' Mika gasped, trying to get his breath. 'Flames, gas, go bang. We could be killed.'

Marikka looked at him as he stood well away from the flames and smoke.

'You said they'd run out of gas,' she protested.

Mika backed away still further, looking around for a fire hose. 'You have to put it out. You can't have a fire on a gas platform. Look at the signs.'

Indeed she had seen the signs.

No Flammable Substances.

No Smoking.

No Naked Flames

There were signs everywhere. But surely the platform wasn't pumping out gas now?

Flakes of burning material floated across the platform towards the main decks and observation deck. The fire was getting a little out of hand.

'We have to signal people we're here, Mika.' Mika found the fire hose, tried to turn it on. It wouldn't budge. 'Help me.'

Reluctantly Marikka joined him. She saw nothing wrong with a fire on the middle of a metal deck that was suspended over the sea. It wasn't going to cause any harm surely.

A gust of wind suddenly blew across the helipad and a shower of sparks shot up into the air behind them. Mika practically pooped himself.

'Oh my god. We have to get it out. We have to put it out. You have no idea how dangerous gas is.'

They turned the heavy brass tap again and a trickle of water came out but no pressure.

'There's buckets of sand in the cabins.' Marikka remembered.

'Go get them!' Mika shouted, coughing as smoke billowed their way, making his eyes water.

Marikka ran off, feeling a little bit guilty now. Mika was certainly spooked. She wondered if he'd ever been in a fire or something.

Mika looked around for lifejackets, liferafts, anything. He had a feeling they'd have to jump into the sea any minute now, if they didn't get blown up first.

'That's an oil or gas platform,' Leon was explaining to Anya. 'Looks pretty old. Doubt it's in use anymore.'

'Is it on fire?'

'I don't think we should get any closer.'

'But it's them. Leon. I know it. They're trying to get our attention.'

'Well, if so, they've got it.' Leon went a little closer, nervous now. They were too close to see the top of the platform, but he could see the sign that stated it was the *Havenmount Gas Rig*. Old and abandoned to be sure, but it definitely shouldn't be on fire.

'There,' Anya pointed, excitement in her voice. 'Look.'

Leon saw the flimsy pontoon tied up by one of the giant gas rig legs.

'Hey? Marikka? Marikka? Can you hear me up there.' Anya screamed.

Up above Marikka thought she heard someone shout her name. 'Now I'm hearing voices.'

She threw the sand on the flames but it hardly affected it. It continued to burn. She realised that the chairs were part plastic and they were going to burn forever.

'**Marikka**?'

Two voices calling now.

Mika was on the far side of the helipad keeping back as far from the flames as he could. He was genuinely scared of being blown up. But the way she saw it, it hadn't blown up yet and she was a lot warmer.

A girl's voice screamed her name again. She had definitely not imagined that.

She ran to the edge and looked down, scared she'd be blown off any second. Smoke billowed across her vision and she saw nothing at first and her eyes watered as she tried to stare.

'Hello?' She shouted back, blind now in the sting of the smoke.

'Marikka?' A man voice called out. 'Down here.'

She rubbed her eyes. There was a small boat down on the water. Two people in it. She whipped around to shout to Mika.

'Mika. Mika. People.'

Mika didn't react at first. He was still wary of the fire.

'Mika. There are people down there.'

Marikka waved to them. Hope surging in her heart. 'We have to go down. I can't jump from here. It's too high.'

Mika hadn't moved.

'Mika there's people down there.'

She ran across to him and grabbed his arm. We have to go lower. We're too high.'

Mika looked at her puzzled. He seemed confused and was coughing in the smoke. 'What are you doing?'

'There's people down there. A boat, Mika. We can escape.'

'And leave the fire?'

'It'll blow itself out.'

Marikka ran down the stairs, nearly slipping on wet metal, heading for the door they'd come up by.

'Come on, help me with the door.'

Mika looked at the smoking fire. He didn't want to leave it, but he didn't want to be left behind either. Reluctantly he ran back down the stairs.

'I can't get it open.' Marikka was saying. Desperation in her voice.

Mika tried to open the door with her, but the handle on this weather side was stuck for sure.

'We can't go this way anyway, remember? The hatch stuck we came through.' Mika reminded her.

Marikka began to panic. What if the rescuers left them? She ran to the railings and waved.

'The door is stuck. We can't get down.' The wind snatched her words away. They couldn't hear her.

'Jump,' the girl was shouting. 'Jump.'

Marikka looked at how far down the boat was. Hitting the sea from this distance would hurt wouldn't it?

Mika was looking back at the smoke on the helipad. They really needed to put that out. It had done it's job. A gust of wind caught the flames it flared up high. Flakes of burning cardboard blew across the deck. Mika winced, tried to stamp them down as burning embers floated towards them.

He joined Marikka on the rails. He saw the boat; saw two people down there. A man and a girl frantically waving.

He was grateful that Marikka's fire had rescued them, but was angry with her for the risk she'd taken.

'We're going to have to jump from here,' he said to Marikka. He tried to calculate the distance. Hitting the sea from this height would be like jumping onto concrete. They had to be almost 30 metres up. He calculated they'd be hitting the water at least sixty miles an hour.

'It could kill us,' Mika told her. 'I mean it.'

'Cliff divers do this all the time and don't die,' Marikka stated, even though she now remembered hating jumping off a diving board only ten metres over the public swimming pool in Scarness. She knew this was going to hurt bad. All her courage disappeared.

'I don't think I can do this.' She confessed. She ran back to the door but it remained jammed.

'We **have** to.' Mika said. 'It's the only choice. We'll go together.'

Behind them an alarm suddenly sounded. The platform wasn't entirely dead after all. The klaxon was deafening and urgent. Mika grabbed Marikka's hand.

'We have to jump now, Marikka. OK? Dive bomb. Hold your legs tight and don't forget to take a deep breath before you hit the water. You'll go deep at that speed.'

Marikka nodded. She was shaking with fear now. All the excitement of being rescued had gone.

'Be a tight ball, then you'll not break anything, understand? Hold your legs. They'll pull you in.'

'Promise you'll jump with me?' Marikka asked.

Mika nodded, taking her hand. 'You have to take a deep breath before you hit the water. Whatever you do, don't panic.'

Marikka crossed herself. She wasn't even religious, but she knew this was going to be the biggest risk she'd ever taken.

Smoke enveloped them again and the alarm continued at a deafening decibel that could probably be heard on the mainland. They climbed over the railings and stood looking down at the water and the two people frantically yelling at them to hurry up and jump.

'Oh my god, I'm going to wet myself,' Marikka said, truly scared. 'Oh my god…'

Mika took her hand again. 'Don't look. Say a prayer.'

'I *am* praying.'

Mika suddenly jumped, his hand still holding Marikka's jerking her away from the platform edge.

Marikka was falling and falling and Mika was screaming at her to wrap herself into a ball and take a breath. She grabbed her feet as the water seemed to rush up towards her so fast it…

Leon and Anya nervously watched them jump. They could hear the alarm screaming from the rig. They kind of expected the whole thing to explode in a fireball any moment, but held their position, ready to zoom in and rescue the jumpers.

Leon manoeuvred the boat to where the kids had landed with a huge splash, plunging deep into the sea.

Mika surfaced first, gasping for air, further from the boat than they had expected. Marikka surfaced seconds later, spitting out water, gasping too, shocked by the cold water.

They got to Mika first. Hauled him out and left him shaking by their feet as they moved towards Marikka.

Leon hauled her in. Leon hardly recognised her, she was so tall and grown from the almost nine-year-old he'd last seen.

Marikka opened her eyes concerned about Mika who hardly stirred beside her, desperately trying to suck in air.

'Mika?'

'I'm OK. I'm OK.' He gasped, spitting out seawater. He looked up at Leon; saw this tall ghost of a man. 'Get us away from here quick mister. Fire on gas platform.'

Leon nodded and turned the little boat heading towards the shore and shallower waters. He had Marikka on board and the miracle of that totally amazed him.

Anya was busy helping Marikka up to a sitting position, getting her settled with her back against the side.

'You're Marikka?'

Marikka nodded, wincing at a sharp pain in her left leg and arm. She was wondering who on earth this strange small girl was and how she knew her name. Marikka looked at the man who'd rescued them and abruptly felt dizzy with shock. It was as if someone had thumped her square in the chest. Her heart literally did a summersault.

'Daddy?' She mouthed. '*Daddy*?' She screamed.

Leon, the ghost, turned to face her and he hardly looked like the man she had known as Daddy, yet impossibly it was him – but he was dead. She looked back at the strange girl and gripped her hand, suddenly full of fear.

'Am I dead? Are we dead?' She asked, tears forming in her eyes.

Anya shook her head and squeezed her hand to reassure her. 'Your father came for you.'

Marikka shook her head violently. 'No, no. no. My father is dead. My father is dead. He died years ago. This is a ghost, a ghost.' She had a coughing fit, spitting out more seawater, then slumped against Anya.

Mika sat up. He was as white as death itself, but semi-conscious at least.

Behind them something went off with a very loud explosion and a giant roaring flame shot up towards the sky from the gas platform.

Marikka briefly stirred, turned her head to look at the huge flame. She immediately felt guilty, glancing over at Mika to whisper. 'I guess they haven't run out of gas after all.'

Then suddenly she flaked out completely.

Anya looked up at Leon, wondering why he hadn't said a word.

'What's your name, boy?' Leon asked Mika.

'Mika.'

'Your lucky day I think.'

Mika knew that. He looked back at the platform. The gas flare was high and bright, but that was all that was burning, the platform itself seemed to be intact.

Leon continued on course. These kids needed to get to a hospital. He sneaked a look at Marikka, scared to even talk to her. She was more beautiful than he had ever hoped she would be. His heart had nearly stopped when he saw her jump from the gas platform. He thought she would die, but here she was, and in the boat with him alive.

'Everything will be fine now', Anya whispered, looking ahead across the sea towards land. 'I'm sure of it.'

THIRTY-FIVE

GRASSLAND

Marikka woke with a start. She was completely disoriented, her hands seemed to be resting on coarse grass and a wind was blowing through the reeds around her. For a moment she stared up at the mist not sure whether it was early morning or twilight. She couldn't make out anything. Aside from the humming of the reeds it was uncannily quiet.

Was she still dreaming?

Where was the raft? Where was Mika?

She sat up, suddenly aware of how cold she was and how thick the mist was swirling around her.

'Where am I?' She croaked. She was suddenly aware her voice sounded wrecked and that her nose was running. She groaned, she had a bloody cold coming. She hated having colds. Her shoes were missing and her clothes were damp. How...?

It all came back like a ton of bricks on top of her head. She'd seen her father. Her dead father. How on earth was that possible?

A hand reached out of the mist and felt her forehead. A young girl's face came into view, a serious look of concern.

'You're awake.'

'Who...?' Marikka struggled to ask. The girl smiled kneeling down beside her.

'He's gone to guide the ambulance. Doesn't think they'll find us in the mist.'

Marikka heard groaning to her left and made out someone under a blanket sleeping on the grass.

'Mika?'

'Let him sleep. He's not well.'

Marikka glanced back at the girl, wondered how old she was. She sounded so mature but couldn't be more than fifteen.

'Who are you? Who went for an ambulance"?

'Anya. Your father went for the ambulance. You've hurt your arm and your leg in the fall. He doesn't want you to try to walk yet.' She smiled again. 'I was so scared for you both when you jumped. So brave.'

Marikka had a memory of falling – of being deathly scared. She remembered the fire on the platform, Mika's anxious face, his sense of panic.

'My father's alive?'

Anya nodded. 'He's been looking for you for a long time.'

Marikka looked away. It made no sense. He was dead. She knew he was dead.

'He's a good man. He set me free,' Anya added, lying down in the grass again. 'I'm so tired now. Very tired.'

Marikka was listening to the wind in the reeds again; they seemed to be playing some odd tune that she couldn't quite grasp. Her father was alive. He had gone to get an ambulance. It didn't make any sense.

'Set you free?' She asked a moment later.

Anya raised one of her legs, the dress fell back to reveal her ugly ankle scars. She heard Marikka draw in breath.

'Like a dog,' Anya said quietly.

Marikka felt her head, she had a nasty bruise on her left side. She wondered when she'd done that. She experimented with her legs and could feel that her left leg was incredibly sore. It was as if she'd fallen onto rocks rather than the sea. Her left arm was stiff as well, she rubbed it wishing she wasn't so bloody cold.

Anya was listening to the seagulls swooping through the mist. It had to be hard for them too in this weather. She could sense Marikka's confusion. She wondered what it must feel like to discover your father, once dead, was still alive. It would be like trying to start the barge engine on a cold morning. It always needed pumping and nursing until it would cough back into life. Yes that was what it must be like. Trying to feel something for someone you thought was dead.

'Have we been here long?' Marikka asked quietly.

Anya wasn't sure but it had to have been at least a couple of hours. Leon had navigated them up a creek, but he wasn't sure where they were and gone to explore. He knew that the ambulance couldn't find them without a postcode and he'd gone in search of the road and someone who knew where they were.

'How did my father even find you?' Marikka was asking.

'He brought me your diary from the fire.'

Marikka stared at Anya. Of all the things to have survived the fire. But why would he show it to this girl? She didn't go to school in Brigstock, she was sure of it. They didn't know each other. Why show *her* the diary?

Anya looked back into the mist. 'They're coming.'

Marikka listened but heard nothing, but thought she glimpsed a blue light.

'Best to try and see if you can walk,' Anya suggested. 'We'll have to walk to the road I think.'

Marikka stood uncertainly, testing her leg. Some pain, but she could walk on it. She didn't think anything was broken. She heard an engine and was encouraged a little.

'You sure that's my father out there?' Marikka asked Anya suddenly.

Anya shrugged. 'Who else would search for you?'

Marikka was thinking the police, any one of her stepfather's dubious friends.

'Don't be afraid,' Anya said softly. 'He's worried you'll reject him.'

'Reject?' Marikka asked, puzzled.

'He's been dead to you for so long.'

Marikka thought suddenly of Deacon – so much was dead to her. Deacon's death was real and the pain in her heart was still there. There wasn't any pain for her father, that had all gone long ago. The man she'd seen in the boat had to be a ghost, definitely a ghost. Then she remembered Mollie. Would he want a daughter who'd plunged little Mollie into the sea, in a sack? How was she ever going to live with this memory? What father would forgive a daughter for doing that?

Someone shouted Anya's name.

'Over here. Over here,' she yelled back.

A figure loomed out of the mist. 'Anya? Marikka?' He still couldn't see them.

'Here,' Anya yelled again and he turned.

Marikka shut her eyes. She didn't want to see him. Didn't want to open her heart. Didn't he know she'd been hurt enough? He had no right to be alive. He was dead. He wouldn't want her anyway. Not now. Not after Mollie.

Two ambulance crewmen in yellow jackets were on them then and they quickly attended to Mika. 'Can't believe you found your way here in this fog,' they were saying to no one in particular.

Marikka opened her eyes. Leon was helping with Mika. Anya grabbed Marikka's arm and squeezed it.

'He's thinking of you.'

Marikka snapped her head around. 'Who?'

'Deacon. He's here somewhere. Says he'll never leave you.'

Marikka felt a fat tear roll down her cheek. She couldn't move. Who on earth was this girl? What was she? How could she know Deacon?

Anya let go and walked towards Leon, leaving Marikka swaying with emotion where she was. None of this was real, but nevertheless she felt suddenly safer. Deacon was here – somewhere – close – even if he was a ghost. He was here keeping her safe.

'Can I help?' She heard herself ask.

'Stay put, Marikka, until they've seen your leg.' Her father ordered her.

Marikka stared at him through the mist. How had he gotten so old? Five years being dead must do that to you she thought. Where had he been? Why had he taken so long to find her?

'It's all right, Marikka. You're safe now. Everything will be all right,' he was saying.

She wished it was but she knew it never could be. A seagull shrieked

– it sounded a lot like the screaming in her head.

She suddenly felt a familiar weight against her leg. *Deacon* she thought looking down. There was nothing there, but she *knew* it was him from the way Deacon always leaned into her, to tell her that he loved her, that he really was there.

They quickly examined her leg and pronounced her OK to walk. They carried Mika to the ambulance. Leon took Marikka's arm and together they followed, going towards the flashing blue light. Anya discretely followed behind noticing that father and daughter didn't speak. Neither one knew what to say to each other. It would take time she figured. It really was like starting that cold barge engine.

THIRTY-SIX

FATHERS & DAUGHTERS

'She looks a lot like you,' the nurse said, noting the similar eyebrows and how dark she was.

'Good looking then,' Dr Silva said with a smile to the nurse. She laughed and moved on. He was looking more closely at the little girl in bed 25. She looked nervous and lost. He studied her admission notes and raised his eyebrows. Broken foot, allegedly chained up for at least last five years. She looked undernourished but remarkably healthy otherwise.

He took out his stethoscope checked her chest and her back, tapping to sound her out.

'Sorry, it's cold I know,' he said when she twitched. 'No sign of any chest infections. That's good. Can you confirm your name and age to me?'

Anya looked at the doctor and sighed. She hadn't wanted to go to hospital at all, she knew it would cause problems, but Leon had insisted.

'Anya.'

'Pretty name. Anya means grace.'

Anya looked at the Doctor and wondered why he was so sad. She had a feeling that his own child was ill or worse.

He was examining her leg and he could barely hide his surprise of what he saw. She had scarring and hard callous marks around where the collar had been clamped around her leg at night. It would take some years to lose the scarring, if ever.

'It doesn't hurt,' she told him.

The doctor just nodded, looking at her broken foot.|

'Who did this to you? Why?'

Anya didn't answer. It was obvious wasn't it? She would have run away if he hadn't chained her up.

Dr Silva made notes on her chart.

'We shall have your foot x-rayed and then, I'm afraid, it will have to be broken again so we can set it straight. I cannot promise it won't hurt.'

'Will I walk normally?'

Dr Silva nodded, taking her hand and pressing it. 'Eventually, yes. You are very brave. I want you to know that you are safe here.'

Anya was feeling his hand, the gold ring on his finger. She felt disturbed. There was something there, something she needed to tell him, but clouded by all the many people he must meet each day. She wanted him to stay, but he was already standing again.

'Do you have a second name, Anya?' He asked casually.

She shook her head. It was ridiculous, but she really didn't remember it. She wasn't even sure Anya was her real name or something Calleigh had forced upon her.

'Like Madonna, only one name huh?' he said, trying to make a joke of it.

She nodded and smiled even if she had never heard of Madonna.

'Who brought you in?'

'Leon. His daughter is over there.' She pointed down the ward to where Marikka slept.

Dr Silva smiled. 'Good, you have a friend here. I am Dr Silva and if you need me you must ask for me, you understand. I will tell the nurses that they are to find me whenever you need me. Is that all right?'

Anya nodded. She wondered why, but she nodded all the same.

She had a sudden thought. The ring. 'Have you been to see me? On the barge?'

Dr Silva looked confused. 'Barge?'

'You have never been to see me on the barge?'

Dr Silva had no idea what she meant, but a nurse was changing a bedpan for a girl in the next bed and suddenly recognised the child Dr

Silva was examining.

'It's the girl who can read objects. My goodness, we have someone famous here, Dr Silva.'

Dr Silva glanced back at the nurse with surprise. 'You know this girl?'

'This is Anya. She helped my mother when my brother went missing.'

Dr Silva was astonished. 'You went to see this girl? This girl who has been chained up for more than five years?' He lifted the gown Anya was wearing and showed the nurse the terrible scarring. The nurse paled, nearly dropping the bedpan. She couldn't speak, looking directly at the doctor for help.

The doctor turned back to Anya. 'You never told anyone?'

Anya shrugged. 'No one helped... till now.'

'And where is the man who chained you? Have the police got him, because I swear I will make sure they...'

Anya just smiled. Leon had taken care of that.

Dr Silva was looking at this girl and thinking she looked so much like his sister Maria when she was young. She could easily be a Portuguese girl. He wondered about her family. She had to have one.

Dr Silva offered a reassuring smile, and squeezed her hand again. 'I want to do some tests on you. Some blood tests. Just as a precaution.' He stood. 'You sure you can't remember your last name?'

Anya was annoyed she couldn't because she was sure that she had tried very hard to commit it to memory. But that had been so long ago. She thought she'd never forget it, but now she had.

'Do blood tests hurt?' She asked quietly.

'No. If we're going to help you, we need to know as much as we can about you.'

He turned to the nurse. 'The man who brought her in?'

'He's talking to the police. He seemed very concerned about this one.'

Dr Silva frowned. They walked away from Anya down the ward a little. Dr Silva questioned the nurse more closely.

'Tell me about your mother. How did she even find this girl?' He asked.

Anya watched them go. She wondered if she should escape now, or wait until dark. She knew from Calleigh that the moment she fished up in a hospital they'd ask questions and he'd told her that they'd never let her go. Lock her up they would. No mother or father to rescue her. She'd be locked up forever. She'd wait till dark, she decided.

Anya woke suddenly. Marikka was at her side, her wrist bandaged, injured in the fall from the gas platform, her hospital pyjamas at least two sizes too large. She had a huge purple bruise on one side of her forehead.

'Good you're awake. I came to thank you.'

Anya put her hand out to Marikka's arm. She knew she'd been through so much. She had no need to thank her.

'I'm glad your father found you.'

Marikka frowned. 'About that. You think he really is my father? He doesn't look much like the man I remember.'

Anya took Marikka's hand. 'I know he is. He told me about his accident and how many operations he had. He is very sure that you are his daughter.' She smiled. 'I think he's scared you don't want a father now.'

Marikka frowned. 'It won't be easy. I told him he has to take Mika too. That boy's growing up wild and he needs a father.'

Anya laughed. 'I think he will do anything you want. Make him go slower on his motorbike though. I was scared to death.'

'That I do remember.' Marikka said smiling briefly, sitting down beside Anya and relaxing. 'He had a terrible old bike he was fixing and one day he took me for a ride. My mother was screaming at him because she said it wasn't safe. I can remember the wind in my face and his warm back and us going 100 mph along a country road.'

Marikka's eyes were closed in remembering. But Anya could tell this was a happy memory.

'Dr Silva was asking questions about you,' Marikka said suddenly. 'He's beautiful. I love his smile. All the kids adore him in this ward.'

Anya smiled. She wondered if she should ask her to escape with her, but then, she'd been found. She had a safe place to go to now.

'And Mika?'

'He's fine. They put him on a drip and they're giving him stronger antibiotics. He'll be back to his annoying self tomorrow, I'm sure. The police are going to question us though. I'm scared stiff. My father says I'm to tell the truth. But I don't think they'll believe me. Luckily they don't know we were on the gas platform and he's not telling.'

Anya could see Marikka was her normal self now. Leon was right; she was beautiful. It was hard to believe that ghost was her father. 'You think the police will want to speak to me?' Anya asked.

'My Dad's got plans for you too. Don't think we're leaving you behind. I know you helped him find me. I walked past that barge you were on the other night. That man who chained you was sleeping on top. Drunk I think.'

Anya nodded. She remembered seeing Marikka going by now. Sensing her troubled mind.

'He said it was the only way he could sleep.'

'We aren't going to let you go. Leon says we'll adopt you and you can go to school and live a normal life.'

Anya winced.

'You don't like?'

'I've never been to school.'

Marikka was appalled. 'Never? Leon says you're very clever though. Taught yourself to read.'

Anya shrugged. It might be true and yes she'd taught herself to read and write, but nevertheless school absolutely terrified her.

'We won't take no for an answer. I always wanted a sister. With your looks we will terrify the local boys.'

Anya looked away. It didn't seem possible that she could be living a normal life with friends and boys.

Leon was suddenly standing there. He placed a newspaper on Anya's bed and opened it to page three.

'This will make you feel better, Anya.'

Anya glanced at the paper and the picture of Calleigh in handcuffs.

'Seems he's wanted for a whole bunch of crimes. Police say he was found in a ditch bound hand and foot. Don't know how that happened.' He winked at her. 'Soon as they fingerprinted him it rang alarm bells at other police stations all the way along the canal. He won't be out of jail for a very long time.'

Anya didn't know why but she felt sorry for her jailer. He'd always boasted that the police couldn't catch him even if they fell on top of him and in a funny way, that was exactly what had happened to him.

Marikka was staring at the newspaper headline – her face a picture of total surprise.

'Oh my god. They found her. They found little Mollie!'

Leon and Anya were staring at her now as she picked up the newspaper and read the news item on the front page.

'Little Mollie. She was kidnapped. The police found her wandering on the A15. She's alive.'

Marikka felt dizzy. So who had been in the sack? Some other kidnapping? Or had she imagined it all. It really had been fish food.

Leon glanced at Marikka. 'You feeling OK? Marikka? Are you all right?

Marikka discovered she was shaking. Mollie was alive. It was all that mattered. She hadn't killed her. She MUST have imagined that there was someone alive in the sack. That was all. A ton of bricks were suddenly lifted off her shoulders. She wasn't a murderer. Nor was Mika. She was taking urgent deep breaths. Her father was resting his hands on her shoulders, a look of real concern on his face. She couldn't tell him about this. Couldn't tell anyone, *ever*. But Mollie was alive. It was if someone had unwrapped huge chains around her lungs. She could breathe again.

Marikka tried to compose herself and offered them both smiles as she let the newspaper drop.

Anya handed her some water and Marikka quickly drank it to cover her embarrassment and elation. She knew they wanted explanations, but she couldn't speak yet. She needed to get herself under control.

She was still unsure about Leon. If she had a choice, having a father who looked healthier and not so emaciated would be hers. She found it very hard to believe he even existed. But she knew now he'd been looking for her for a very long time. The fact that he'd actually tied up this man who'd hurt and imprisoned Anya said a great deal. You had to respect a man who'd do that to save a girl.

'You think we'll be happy?' Marikka asked him suddenly.

'We will have to work at it. I don't live in a big house. I have very little actually. Your mother saw to that.'

She shrugged. 'I don't care. I lost everything I care about anyway.'

'Did you have a lot of things?'

She shook her head. 'No, but I had a dog who loved me enough to save my life. Deacon will always be my hero.'

'Deacon? That's a good name for a dog. I have of photo of you and him. He was very handsome.'

Marikka nodded. 'I'll never have anyone as faithful as him, never. He was naughty too. But I loved that about him.'

Leon looked at this strong brave beautiful girl and wondered if was too late to come into her life, to try to fill all the gaps. He wondered what her connection was to this Mollie Pendleton who'd been found alive.

'I need to go and sign a statement with the police in Brigstock. I don't remember when I last slept.' He told them both.

'I have to see Mika.' Marikka declared suddenly. 'He doesn't want to go to school,' she told him. 'He wants to be an apprentice. He's mad about cars and machines. He's a natural with machines. He wants to do a special course at Silverstone.'

Leon took that on board. 'Is Mika your boyfriend?'

'God no, he's only a kid. Any girl who falls for Mika will have to know a lot about cars, that's all I can say.'

Leon smiled, puzzled about the relationship between the boy and his daughter, but loved the fact that she was still the same girl, always concerned about others.

'OK. Go see him. Reassure him that he's not in trouble, all right? Detective Barber has promised me that. I have to go to Brigstock now. Got to collect my bike too. I'll be back to see you both later. Please take care of each other, OK? I don't want any more surprises.'

Leon was reluctant to go, as if they both would disappear the moment he turned his back. 'I'll be back. I promise.'

Marikka watched him go and wished she'd made an effort to give him a hug or something. He'd been nothing but kind. But it was just so hard to think of him as her father.

A nurse came to Anya's bed armed with lots of needles. She smiled as Anya hid her face behind her hands.

'I'm just going to take some blood samples, Anya.'

Anya looked stricken and reached for Marikka's hand.

'Don't worry. I'll stay with you,' she said.

Anya turned away as the nurse swabbed her arm to take the samples. She hated needles. Marikka made faces to distract her and almost got her to laugh.

'There, see? Didn't hurt did it?'

Anya still didn't look. She didn't want to see the vials full of her blood.

'Have a rest,' the nurse told her, 'they'll be bringing lunch around soon.'

Marikka waited for the nurse to leave then took Anya's hand again. 'Come on, Mika's in a room all on his own. Let's go and annoy him.'

Anya nodded and laughed, pushing away the bedclothes, momentarily feeling dizzy from the blood they'd taken. She didn't want to be in this bed anyway.

'Dr Silva asked me my name,' Anya told Marikka as they walked towards the ward doors. 'I couldn't remember it. My surname. It's gone. I definitely remember trying to remember it when I was young. Is that crazy?'

'I'm just surprised you're sane. You'll remember it.'

'I will?'

'Of course. You blocked it, that's all. I blocked everything to do with my father. The moment my mother told me he was dead I decided to forget him. I have no idea why. The therapist said I was trying not to feel anything because it hurt so much. I was nine. I was so stupidly unhappy. Discovering he was dead made me really angry, because I'd built up this whole fantasy that one day he was going to rescue me from my evil mother, and now he wouldn't be able to. So I just blocked him out.'

Anya screwed up her face and sensed that there was truth in what Marikka said. She had forgotten her own mother's face. Forgotten her mother's name, but not quite forgotten that she had sold her to Calleigh. She felt a sudden flash of anger. How could anyone do that?

'I had a name. I know I did,' she said fiercely, 'and it wasn't Anya.'

Marikka took her arm and squeezed it. 'Anya is a cute name. Don't fret about it.'

Mika was reading a car magazine. He looked happy to see them both.

'Did you hear, Marikka? They found Mollie. They found that girl.'

Marikka nodded. Knew instantly that it had meant the same to him as her. Didn't exactly explain *what* was in the sack, but at least it hadn't been that little girl. She exchanged secret glances with him. It was over. It didn't have to haunt either of them ever again. They didn't need to talk about it either.

'About time you guys came to see me.' Mika told them, coughing, his voice very scratchy. He had new stitches on his cheek, but they weren't too noticeable, certainly neater than the ones on his legs. He was on a saline drip, but the colour had returned to his face and his eyes were almost normal again. His chest hurt when he coughed, but he knew he was lucky to be alive.

Marikka grinned and jumped on his bed, she pulled Anya after her. 'We're here to save you from terminal boredom.'

'I didn't say thanks, Anya.' Mika croaked. 'We wouldn't have been saved if it wasn't for you.'

Anya blushed.

Marikka nodded and gave her another huge hug.

'You're amazing actually. My father must really think you're…'

'Weird?' Anya said, laughing to cover her embarrassment. Mika was staring at her and she felt embarrassed. 'I didn't do much,' Anya muttered.

Mika shook his head. 'You're amazing. The nurses have been talking about you. I wish I could give you something to say thanks.'

Anya smiled. 'Like the silver broach?'

Mika was astonished. 'You have it?'

'I put it back in the sea. It belongs there.'

Marikka looked at Mika sharply, but he didn't mock Anya.

'I was so excited when I found it, I didn't think about where it came from.'

'It's all right. It's back there now with Rose.'

Marikka studied this tiny girl and wanted to protect her. She took everything so seriously.

Mika turned to Marikka. 'They said my stitches were pretty good. I got metal poisoning. Can you believe that?' Mika said. 'Might not even be the crash that made me sick. Something back at the yard must have contaminated me.'

'I'm not surprised.' Marikka said, adding. 'Jackson's disappeared.'

'He'll be in Spain.' Mika said confidently, turning a moment to cough and wipe his mouth. 'He was always talking about Spain and how hard it was to find anyone there. You think your father's OK with me coming home with you?'

'I think he wants you more than me. You have any idea how many hours he spends rebuilding engines.'

Mika grinned.

Anya felt safe with Marikka at her side. But if she ran now she'd never see her again. But then again, if she didn't run social services would come for sure. Calleigh had told her what would happen. They'd lock her up as a freak. Social services hated freaks.

A nurse was hovering at the door. She was biting her lip, unsure of what to say. Anya knew that look.

'Did you want to talk to me?' She asked. The nurse nodded,

relieved Anya had spoken first.

'I have something. Would you read it?'

Anya sighed. She guessed she'd forever be the girl who read objects.

'Here?' Anya asked, embarrassed to be doing this in front of the others now.

The nurse beckoned her and Anya followed.

'Don't go far. I'm looking after you,' Marikka called after her.

Anya looked back and smiled, actually appreciating that Marikka cared.

The nurse led her to an empty room with an examining bed in it. 'We'll be private in here. Dr Silva told us to watch over you. He doesn't want you to leave.'

Anya was puzzled. 'Why?'

'He's taken a shine to you, I reckon. No reward in pleasing kids I tell him, but he just shakes his head.'

Anya said nothing. She'd barely spoken to the doctor, but she was glad he was looking out for her. That made two people. Calleigh was wrong. He'd said no one would ever want a freak and cripple. There was no fixing the freak, but if she could walk properly again... 'What do you want me to look at?'

'It's my boyfriend's. There's something going on. The girls told me you could read stuff. Tell me if he's true.'

Anya looked at her with steady professional eyes.

'Sometimes people don't want to know the truth. They get angry...'

The nurse held up her hands. 'I want to know the truth.' Her eyes began to water. 'No matter what.'

Anya put her hand out for the object and a wallet was placed in her hands. Soft expensive leather. It told of many things. She closed her eyes and went to work.

Anya waited till eleven o'clock that night. The hospital was quieter, the children's ward was not quite dark. Nurses still flitted by from time to time checking on them. She always found it hard to sleep unless it was completely dark. She had to make a decision. Leave now and chance never having her foot fixed or risk social services finding her. She was already out of bed, hunting for her clothes in the tiny beside locker.

'Ola.'

She looked up, saw Dr Silva there. He wasn't wearing his doctor's clothes just a jerkin and jogging pants. He looked hot and sweaty as if he'd run there.

'What are you doing?'

'I have no slippers. I have to go to the…' Anya lied.

Dr Silva smiled. 'You can go barefoot. Don't worry. They clean the floor here quite often, I hear.'

Nervously Anya moved off to the nearby bathroom, almost running she was so scared. Had he guessed what she was doing? How could she run now, with him there? How long would he stay?

He was still there sitting beside her bed when she returned, so she got back into bed.

'I heard you made a nurse cry.'

Anya hung her head. 'I'm sorry. I only told her the truth.'

'That her boyfriend was cheating on her.'

Anya nodded; she felt she should explain. 'No. Not cheating *on* her. He was cheating her. Taking her money.'

'Turns out, that this little girl who can read objects, was correct. She discovered he'd forged her signature and borrowed a lot of money in her name. She is very upset.'

Anya didn't know what to do. She felt upset herself. She hadn't even wanted to tell the nurse.

'She told me that she wants to make sure that I tell you that she's very grateful to you. She said you are truly gifted.'

'I don't think it's a gift.'

'Oh, but it is. A true gift. My grandmother had a gift. She could tell you anything about the weather. Whether it was going to rain or be hot. Farmers used to call her up and ask her if it was a good week to plant or harvest. No one in my village would do anything without consulting her. She was always right.'

Anya smiled glad to hear the story and know there were other freaks out there like her. She loved the way Dr Silva spoke. So soft and gentle and he seemed to be telling the truth. He wouldn't make such a thing up would he?

Anya suddenly remembered something. 'I think I remembered my name, my real name.'

Dr Silva frowned. 'You're sure?'

'Well, no. Not the exact name. I just remembered I was called after my Grandmother.'

Dr Silva seemed pleased by that.

'But I don't know what she was called. Is that stupid?'

Dr Silva put his head to one side and smiled. 'It's a start. I have the results of your blood test here.'

Anya looked at him blankly. She didn't know what it meant.

'The good news is that you are pretty healthy considering. Under weight, undersized, but nothing that eating more regularly and some exercise won't fix. We can operate on your foot very soon and start treatment on your scarring too.'

Anya waited. She knew there was something else.

'The bad news is not really bad news because it has a silver lining. If that makes any sense.' He laughed nervously, checking his watch and looking over to ward entrance doors.

'Bad news?' Anya asked.

'Hypoglycaemia. Low blood sugar. I suspect caused by your diet. There is a serious iron deficiency. Don't worry. We can treat this. Don't look so sad.'

Out of the corners of her eyes Anya saw someone coming into the children's ward being led by a nurse who deposited him at the end of her bed. Dr Silva was still speaking but she'd stopped listening. He was telling her that they were going to treat her, she would have to take pills, but she didn't want to hear this. She didn't want to be sick. Didn't want anything except to...

The stranger, a very nervous man was talking to Dr Silva now. He looked as though he'd come there in a hurry. They were shaking hands. Anya shook herself. She ought to listen, they were both looking at her as if expecting an answer.

'You see. We took your blood today Anya and then because it had so many unusual aspects to it, I asked other hospitals if anyone else had your blood type. Everything is connected now and that's when we found Senor Medeiros.'

'Ola,' the small dark Portuguese man said.

'She doesn't speak Portuguese,' Dr Silva muttered to the man. Then he smiled at Anya. 'He lives in Leeds. He's got the same blood problems as you. So you can see, he's fine and healthy.'

Anya nodded. Not at all sure where this was all going and why it was so important she should see a total stranger.

Marikka further down the ward was awake and watching, curious as to what was happening to Anya. She couldn't hear much because they were whispering. It made her anxious for her and she got out of bed, pulling her dressing gown on.

The stranger took out a small book, a child's book from a rucksack and Anya could see he was desperate for her to look at it, yet just as desperate for her not to. Whatever it was, it was very precious to him.

'I have another test...' Dr Silva began.

Anya put her hand out for the book. 'I know this test, Doctor. I have been doing this test all my life.'

Dr Silva shook his head. 'I promise you that this is the only test I will ever do like this, Anya. I promise. It is not a trick.'

Anya knew what it was without touching it. The man's long dead daughter's book. It had to be. Nothing else was as precious to him as that. She knew now why the doctor had let him come at night when there was no one to witness it.

Anya held her hand out but still he didn't give it to her.

'Do you believe in fate?' The man asked her.

Anya smiled. 'Fate is all we have,' she replied. 'I will tell you the truth. I can only tell the truth. Please don't be angry with me if I say something you don't want to hear.'

Senor Medeiros looked away a moment, clearly emotional. 'I am afraid. The impossibility of it, that's what I can't believe, the sheer impossibility.'

Anya didn't understand him. She thought he didn't want to know that his daughter was dead. The book might not even say that. The girl had been gone years most likely. The book may have broken the connection. She didn't want to disappoint him. She didn't want to break his heart, she didn't really want to pick up the book at all.

It lay between them, a dead weight, though it could only be a few thick pages of paper. Anya took a deep breath and picked it up, placing the closed book firmly between both hands, waiting for the messages and the truth to come.

Instead she suddenly froze. Tears filled her eyes, she began to moan.

Dr Silva began to look alarmed, glancing at the stranger who stared at Anya with a mixture of hope and fear, his hands shaking.

Marikka began to move closer. This wasn't right. They couldn't use Anya like this. Doctor, or no. It wasn't right. Hadn't she suffered enough?

Anya tried to speak, the words could hardly come out, her lips trembled. Dr Silva looked at her with concern, glancing around the ward in case she woke anyone. He didn't notice Marikka approaching behind him.

'This is my book,' Anya whispered hoarsely, tears flowing down her cheeks now. Louder now. 'This is MY BOOK. My first book. My book.'

It was all she could say. Her hands shook, she opened the first page and read

'This Book belongs to Ynez Medeiros.'

Anya gasped. It was if a flood had just engulfed her and she was carried away by the rush of water.

'My book...' she repeated, looking at the stranger who was crying now, visibly shaking, a hand reaching out to her.

Marikka ran to Anya's side. Dr Silva couldn't move he was so overcome. Senor Medeiros swayed on his feet.

'He's your father, Anya? This man is your father?'

Marikka pulled Anya out of her sitting position and brought father and daughter together. They were both crying, in wonder and amazement at the impossibility of it all.

'The blood tests.' Dr Silva gasped, needing to explain something to Marikka.

Marikka understood now.

'My name is Ynez,' Anya told Marikka sucking in breath and trying not to cry. 'I have a father.'

Marikka hugged her. Father found daughter. It was a miracle. She was crying too.

Marikka finally couldn't bear it. She couldn't explain. She was suddenly overcome with an incredible sadness. She broke away and ran. Ran out through the heavy double doors of the ward. Ran down the endless corridors, ran down the stairs, and more stairs and burst through more heavy doors into the hospital lobby and she was going to run further but stopped, red eyed, still sobbing because there in the lobby, sleeping across three chairs, right under the nose of the night porter who was reading a book under a dim light, was her father.

Leon was slumped on the chairs, exhausted, but here. She collapsed in a heap beside him, unable to stop her tears. He woke suddenly and nearly fell off the chairs. Marikka almost laughed and then, finally, for the first time, was in his arms and he was holding her, bewildered, shocked, happy as she cried in hospital pyjamas in the stupid hospital lobby.

'Thank you for finding me. Thank you for never forgetting me,' Marikka whispered. 'I let you die. I didn't want to believe you were dead, but I let you die and you must forgive me, Daddy. Please forgive me. I didn't mean to let you die.'

Leon held her tight. He had no idea what had brought this on, but he was very glad he had come back to the hospital to sleep. He had had a terrible thought that he'd never see her again if he didn't come back.

'You were always alive for me. You were why I lived, Marikka. After my crash and I had to learn to walk again, I did it for you.'

A night shift nurse walked by. She most likely thought someone had died. She could never have guessed that this was what real happiness looked like. Never knew that Anya had been claimed, Marikka had been saved.

Leon held her as Marikka cried for all that was lost. Deacon, Monday, and all the stupidity in the world. She cried for a father who had searched for her for years and finally found her.

No one disturbed them. At some point Leon took her back upstairs and stayed there until she slept again. Dr Silva passed by, nodded in acknowledgment. He seemed to have been crying too. Leon wondered if a child had died, but was glad to see Anya was curled up asleep in her bed.

Dr Silva paused in his steps a moment.

'You have a place to sleep, Mr Stillwater?'

Leon shrugged. 'I …'

Dr Silva put out his hand to Leon. 'Come with me. Giving you a bed for the night, is the very least I can do to say thank you.'

'Thank?'

'Anya. The little girl who read objects is found, Mr Stillwater. You are God's instrument, yes? You brought her here. You made me look at her. I found her father was being treated for the same problems in Leeds. Like you, he has looked for his Inez for years. I will never forget you, Mr Stillwater. Never.'

Leon followed the Doctor out of the ward bemused. He had just being trying to find his Marikka. He was happy things had turned out well.

'Come. We shall drink brandy and celebrate life's mysteries.' Dr Silva said with a smile.

They left together. Tomorrow would bring more worries, but for today it was enough there should be a moment to be happy.

FIN

ABOUT THE AUTHOR

Sam Hawksmoor lives and writes in a cold drafty tower overlooking the bleak North Sea coast. He has written many novels over the years and is a former University Senior Lecturer – having run the Post-Grad Creative Writing Programmes at Falmouth and Portsmouth Universities. In addition he has been running an on-line writers magazine www.hackwriters.com for around 16 years

The YA novels by Sam Hawksmoor: www.samhawksmoor.com
The Repossession (Hodder)
(Winner of The Wirral 'Paperback of the Year' 2013)
The Hunting (Hodder)
The Heaviness (Hammer & Tong)
The Repercussions of Tomas D (Hammer & Tong)
Another Place to Die: The Endtime Chronicles

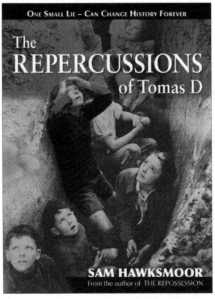

The Repercussions of Tomas D
'Terrific fast paced read. Highly
recommend for teens / YA / and adults too!'
Carine on Goodreads.com

THE REPOSSESSION TRILOGY

The Repossession *(Part 1)*
Winner of The Wirral
'Paperback of the Year' 2013

The Hunting *(Part 2)*

The Heaviness (Part 3)

Another place to Die: The Endtime Chronicles

'Beautiful, plausible, and sickeningly addictive, Another Place to Die will terrify you, thrill you, and make you petrified of anyone who comes near you...' Roxy Williams - Amazon.co.uk